THE HAUNTED LADY

MARY ROBERTS RINEHART (1876-1958) was the most beloved and best-selling mystery writer in America in the first half of the twentieth century. Born in Pittsburgh, Rinehart trained as a nurse and married a doctor. When a stock market crash sent the young couple into debt, Rinehart leaned on her writing—previously a part-time occupation—to pay the bills. Credited with inventing the phrase, "The butler did it"—a phrase she never actually wrote—Rinehart is often called an American Agatha Christie, even though she was much more popular during her heyday.

OTTO PENZLER, the creator of American Mystery Classics, is also the founder of the Mysterious Press (1975), a literary crime imprint now associated with Grove/Atlantic; Mysterious Press. com (2011), an electronic-book publishing company; and New York City's Mysterious Bookshop (1979). He has won a Raven, the Ellery Queen Award, two Edgars (for the *Encyclopedia of Mystery and Detection*, 1977, and *The Lineup*, 2010), and lifetime achievement awards from NoirCon and *The Strand Magazine*. He has edited more than 70 anthologies and written extensively about mystery fiction.

THE HAUNTED
LADY

MARY ROBERTS
RINEHART

Introduction by
OTTO
PENZLER

AMERICAN
MYSTERY
CLASSICS

Penzler Publishers
New York

Published in 2020 by Penzler Publishers
58 Warren Street, New York, NY 10007
penzlerpublishers.com

Distributed by W. W. Norton

Cover image: Andy Ross
Cover design: Mauricio Diaz

Paperback ISBN 9781613161609
Hardcover ISBN 9781613161593

Library of Congress Control Number: 2019920294

Printed in the United States of America

9 8 7 6 5 4 3 2 1

THE HAUNTED LADY

INTRODUCTION

DURING WHAT is often called the Golden Age of mystery fiction, the years between the two World Wars, one of the best-selling writers in America was Mary Roberts Rinehart. Not just a best-selling mystery writer—a bestselling *writer*, period. The list of the top ten bestselling books for each year in the 1920s showed Rinehart on the list five times, an impressive feat matched only by Sinclair Lewis. The only mystery titles that outsold her in those years were *Rebecca* by Daphne du Maurier and two titles by S.S. Van Dine, *The Greene Murder Case* and *The Bishop Murder Case*.

In many regards, Mary Roberts Rinehart was the American Agatha Christie, both in terms of popularity and productivity. Like her British counterpart, the prolific Rinehart wrote a large number of bestselling mysteries, short stories, straight novels, and stage plays, some of which were hugely successful—especially 1920's *The Bat*.

Unlike Christie, however, Rinehart's popularity waned after her death in 1958. One cause of this decreased interest was likely the lack of a long-running series character, which would have given new readers an easy entry-point into her work (although Miss Letitia Carberry, known as Tish, appeared in several books, and Nurse Adams, dubbed "Miss Pinkerton" by the police for her uncanny ability to become embroiled in criminal activities, had a few appearances). At the same time, reading tastes in the United States were changing towards the end of her career, tending towards more straightforward detection; while Christie's detectives, notably Hercule Poirot, were reasoning creatures largely lacking in emotions, Rinehart's characters were swept up in the very human responses of romance, curiosity, fear, and tenacity.

Furthermore, many of the characteristics that made Rinehart's writing so unique and exciting in its day became hackneyed by writers seeking to cash in on the popularity of her style; as a result, her work, though it retains the mark of originality, was all but forgotten in the ensuing flood of half-rate imitations.

For example, a common element in Rinehart's mysteries was the author's penchant for moving the storyline along with foreshadowing. While this is a frequently used device in contemporary literature, Rinehart often employed a method that has become mocked by some, partially because of its simplicity: the statement (and its numerous variations) "had I but known then what I know now, this could have been avoided," often creeps into her books—so commonly, in fact, that Rinehart's use of the contrivance is famously credited (or blamed, depending on your point of view) for creating the entire "Had-I-But-Known" school of fiction.

Rinehart's protagonists typically exhibit very poor judgment. Warned never—*never*—to enter the basement under any circumstances, for instance, they are absolutely certain to be found there within the next few pages, only to be rescued at the very last instant. The characters—almost exclusively female, with a few exceptions—often have flashes of insight that come moments too late to prevent another murder.

Born to a poor family in Pittsburgh, the author's father committed suicide just as she was graduating from nursing school, where she had met Dr. Stanley Marshall Rinehart, who she married in 1896 at the age of twenty. They had three sons. Because of poor investments, the young nurse and her doctor husband struggled financially so she began to write, selling forty-five stories in the first year (1903). The editor of *Munsey's Magazine* suggested that she write a novel, which he would serialize, and she quickly produced *The Man in Lower Ten*, followed immediately by *The Circular Staircase*, which was published in book form first, in 1908. She was a consistent best-seller from that point on. After her husband died in 1932, Mary Roberts Rinehart, now a fabulously wealthy woman from the sales of her books, moved into a luxurious, eighteen-room Park Avenue apartment where she lived alone for the rest of her life.

Rinehart's mysteries have a surprisingly violent side to them (though never graphically described), with the initial murder serving as a springboard to subsequent multiple murders. Her tales are unfailingly filled with sentimental love stories and gentle humor, both unusual elements of crime fiction in the early decades of the twentieth century.

Describing some of her books, Rinehart displayed her sly sense of humor while conceding the levels of violence and the body count are not entirely expected from an author known for her romantic and heart-warming mystery fiction. Here are some selected titles about which she warned readers:

The After House (1914): "I killed three people with one axe, raising the average number of murders per crime book to a new high level."

The Album (1933): "The answer to four gruesome murders lies in a dusty album for everyone to see."

The Wall (1938): "I commit three shocking murders in a fashionable New England summer colony."

The Great Mistake (1940): "A murder story set in the suburbs, involving a bag of toads, a pair of trousers and some missing keys."

The present book, *The Haunted Lady*, first published in 1942, features Nurse Adams, the same protagonist as her earlier, more famous book, *Miss Pinkerton*, published a decade earlier. When the elderly Eliza Fairbanks goes to the police with bizarre complaints, Inspector Fuller calls on Adams to investigate the situation in the old mansion.

While most everyone thinks Miss Fairbanks is batty, Adams learns that someone has released rats and bats in her room in an apparent attempt to frighten her to death. A more straightforward attempt, arsenic in her sugar bowl, had failed. Other strange events occur in this wonderfully atmospheric novel: a radio that seems to turn itself on in the middle of the night, window screens that inexplicably are removed from the windows, and even fresh coats of paint at the windows.

Many of the elements that Rinehart frequently employed in her novels are here: eccentric characters, a creepy old house, a rich old woman in grave danger, a pair of young lovers, and an amateur sleuth who assists the baffled police. But *The Haunted Lady* adds an element that made no appearance in any of her other works—a locked room mystery. In a room that has been completely safeguarded (doors and windows locked, no secret entrances, no access through a fireplace or any other opening), the victim, alone, is stabbed to death.

Although some of the mores and social niceties of her time have changed, Rinehart's greatest strengths as a writer were her ability to tell a story that compelled the reader to turn the page, and to create universal characters to which all of us can relate. That ability never goes out of style and, as long as people read books, neither will Mary Roberts Rinehart, the universally beloved writer who, for two decades, was the best-paid writer in America.

—OTTO PENZLER

1.

Hilda Adams was going through her usual routine after coming off a case. She had taken a long bath, using plenty of bath salts, shampooed her short, slightly graying hair, examined her feet and cut her toenails, and was now carefully rubbing hand lotion into her small but capable hands.

Sitting there in her nightgown she looked rather like a thirty-eight-year-old cherub. Her skin was rosy, her eyes clear, almost childish. That appearance of hers was her stock in trade, as Inspector Fuller had said to the new commissioner that same day.

"She looks as though she still thought the stork brought babies," he said. "That's something for a woman who has been a trained nurse for fifteen years. But she can see more with those blue eyes of hers than most of us could with a microscope. What's more, people confide in her. She's not the talking sort, so they think she's safe. She sits and knits and tells them about her canary bird at home, and pretty soon they're pouring out all they know. It's a gift."

"Pretty useful, eh?"

"Useful! I'll say. What's the first thing the first families think of when there's trouble? A trained nurse. Somebody cracks, and there you are. Or there she is."

"I shouldn't think the first families would have that kind of trouble."

The inspector looked at the new commissioner with a faintly patronizing smile.

"You'd be surprised," he said. "They have money, and money breeds trouble. Not only that. Sometimes they have bats."

He grinned. The new commissioner stared at him suspiciously.

"Fact," said the inspector. "Had an old woman in this afternoon who says she gets bats in her bedroom. Everything closed up, but bats just the same. Also a rat now and then, and a sparrow or two."

The commissioner raised his eyebrows.

"No giant panda?" he inquired. "No elephants?"

"Not so far. Hears queer noises, too."

"Sounds haunted," said the commissioner. "Old women get funny sometimes. My wife's mother used to think she saw her dead husband. She'd never liked him. Threw things at him."

The inspector smiled politely.

"Maybe. Maybe not. She had her granddaughter with her. The girl said it was true. I gathered that the granddaughter made her come."

"What was the general idea?"

"The girl wanted an officer in the grounds at night. It's the Fairbanks place. Maybe you know it. She seemed to think somebody gets in the house at night and lets in the menagerie. The old lady said that was nonsense; that the trouble was in the house itself."

The commissioner looked astounded.

"You're not talking about Eliza Fairbanks?"

"We're not on first-name terms yet. It's Mrs. Fairbanks, relict of one Henry Fairbanks, if that means anything to you."

"Good God," said the commissioner feebly. "What about it? What did you tell her?"

The inspector got up and shook down the legs of his trousers.

"I suggested a good reliable companion; a woman to keep her comfortable as well as safe." He smiled. "Preferably a trained nurse. The old lady said she'd talk to her doctor. I'm waiting to hear from him."

"And you'll send the Adams woman?"

"I'll send Miss Adams, if she's free," said the inspector, with a slight emphasis on the "Miss." "And if Hilda Adams says the house is haunted, or that the entire city zoo has moved into the Fairbanks place, I'll believe her."

He went out then, grinning, and the commissioner leaned back in the chair behind his big desk and grunted. He had enough to do without worrying about senile old women, even if the woman was Eliza Fairbanks. Or was the word "anile"? He wasn't sure.

The message did not reach the inspector until eight o'clock that night. Then it was not the doctor who called. It was the granddaughter.

"Is that Inspector Fuller?" she said.

"It is."

The girl seemed slightly breathless.

"I'm calling for my grandmother. She said to tell you she has caught another bat."

"Has she?"

"Has she what?"

"Caught another bat."

"Yes. She has it in a towel. I slipped out to telephone. She doesn't trust the servants or any of us. She wants you to send somebody. You spoke about a nurse today. I think she should have someone tonight. She's pretty nervous."

The inspector considered that.

"What about the doctor?"

"I've told him. He'll call you soon. Doctor Brooke. Courtney Brooke."

"Fine," said the inspector, and hung up.

Which was why, as Hilda Adams finished rubbing in the hand lotion that night, covered her canary, and was about to crawl into her tidy bed, her telephone rang.

She looked at it with distaste. She liked an interval between her cases, to go over her uniforms and caps, to darn her stockings—although the way stockings went today they were usually beyond darning—and to see a movie or two. For a moment she was tempted to let it ring. Then she lifted the receiver.

"Hello," she said.

"Fuller speaking. That Miss Pinkerton?"

"This is Hilda Adams," she said coldly. "I wish you'd stop that nonsense."

"Gone to bed?"

"Yes."

"Well, that's too bad. I've got a case for you."

"Not tonight you haven't," said Hilda flatly.

"This will interest you, Hilda. Old lady has just caught a bat in her room. Has it in a towel."

"Really? Not in her hair? Or a butterfly net?"

"When I say towel I mean towel," said the inspector firmly. "She seems to have visits from a sort of traveling menagerie—birds, bats, and rats."

"I don't take mental cases, and you know it, inspector. Besides, I've just come off duty."

The inspector was exasperated.

"See here, Hilda," he said. "This may be something or it may be nothing. But it looks damned queer to me. Her granddaughter was with her, and she says it's true. She'll call you pretty soon. I want you to take the case. Be a sport."

Hilda looked desperately about her, at the covered birdcage, at her soft bed, and through the door to her small sitting-room with its chintz-covered chairs, its soft blue curtains, and its piles of unread magazines. She even felt her hair, which was still slightly damp.

"There are plenty of bats around this time of year," she said. "Why shouldn't she catch one?"

"Because there is no possible way for it to get in," said the inspector. "Be a good girl, Hilda, and keep those blue eyes of yours open."

She agreed finally, but without enthusiasm, and when a few minutes later a young and troubled voice called her over the telephone, she was already packing her suitcase. The girl was evidently following instructions.

"I'm telephoning for Doctor Brooke," she said. "My grandmother isn't well. I'm terribly sorry to call you so late, but I don't think she ought to be alone tonight. Can you possibly come?"

"Is this the case Inspector Fuller telephoned about?"

The girl's voice sounded constrained.

"Yes," she said.

"All right. I'll be there in an hour. Maybe less."

Hilda thought she heard a sigh of relief.

"That's splendid. It's Mrs. Henry Fairbanks. The address is Ten Grove Avenue. I'll be waiting for you."

Hilda hung up and sat back on the edge of her bed. The name had startled her. So old Eliza Fairbanks was catching bats in towels, after years of dominating the social life of the city. Lady Fairbanks, they had called her in Hilda's childhood, when the Henry Fairbanks place still had the last iron deer on its front lawn, and an iron fence around it to keep out *hoi polloi*. The deer was gone now, and so was Henry. Even the neighborhood had changed. It was filled with bleak boardinghouses, and a neighborhood market was on the opposite corner. But the big square house still stood in its own grounds surrounded by its fence, as though defiant of a changing neighborhood and a changing world.

She got up and began to dress. Perhaps in deference to her memories she put on her best suit and a new hat. Then, canary cage in one hand and suitcase in the other, she went down the stairs. At her landlady's door she uncovered the cage. The bird was excited. He was hopping from perch to perch, but when he saw her he was quiet, looking at her with sharp, beadlike eyes.

"Be good, Dicky," she said. "And mind you take your bath every day."

The bird chirped and she re-covered him. She thought rather drearily that she lived vicariously a good many lives, but very little of her own, including Dicky's. She left the cage, after her usual custom, with a card saying where she had gone. Then, letting herself quietly out of the house, she walked to the taxi stand at the corner. Jim Smith, who often drove her, touched his cap and took her suitcase.

"Thought you just came in," he said conversationally.

"So I did, Jim. Take me to Ten Grove Avenue, will you?"

He looked at her quickly.

"Somebody sick at the Fairbanks?"

"Old Mrs. Fairbanks isn't well."

Jim laughed.

"Been seeing more bats, has she?"

"Bats? Where did you hear that?"

"Things get around," said Jim cheerfully.

Hilda sat forward on the edge of the seat. Without her night-gown and with her short hair covered she had lost the look of a thirty-eighty-year-old cherub and become a calm and efficient spinster, the sort who could knit and talk about her canary at home, while people poured out their secrets to her. She stared at Jim's back.

"What *is* all this talk about Mrs. Fairbanks, Jim?"

"Well, she's had a lot of trouble, the old lady. And she ain't so young nowadays. The talk is that she's got softening of the brain; thinks she's haunted. Sees bats in her room, and all sorts of things. What I say is if she wants to see bats, let her see them. I've known 'em to see worse."

He turned neatly into the Fairbanks driveway and stopped with a flourish under the porte-cochere at the side of the house. Hilda glanced about her. The building looked quiet and normal; just a big red brick block with a light in the side hall and one or two scattered above. Jim carried her suitcase up to the door and put it down there.

"Well, good luck to you," he said. "Don't let that talk bother you any. It sounds screwy to me."

"I'm not easy to scare," said Hilda grimly.

She paid him and saw him off before she rang the bell, but she felt rather lonely as the taxi disappeared. There was something wrong if the inspector wanted her on the case. And he definitely did not believe in ghosts. Standing there in the darkness she remembered the day Mrs. Fairbanks's daughter Marian had been married almost twenty years ago. She had been a probationer at the hospital then, and she had walked past the place on her off-duty. There had been a red carpet over these steps then, and a crowd kept outside the iron fence by a policeman was looking in excitedly. She had stopped and looked, too.

The cars were coming back from the church, and press photographers were waiting. When the bride and groom arrived they had stopped on the steps, and now, years later, Hilda still remembered that picture—Marian in white satin and veil, with a long train caught up in one hand, while the other held her bouquet of white orchids; and the groom, tall and handsome, a gardenia in the lapel of his morning coat, smiling down at her.

To the little probationer outside on the pavement it had been pure romance, Marian and Frank Garrison, clad in youth and beauty that day. And it had ended in a divorce.

She turned abruptly and rang the doorbell.

2.

SHE WAS surprised when a girl opened the door. She had expected a butler, or at least a parlormaid. It was the girl who had telephoned her, as she knew when she spoke.

"I suppose you are Miss Adams?"

Hilda was aware that the girl was inspecting her. She smiled reassuringly.

"Yes."

"I'm Janice Garrison. I'm so glad you came." She looked around, as if she was afraid of being overheard. "I've been frightfully worried."

She led the way along the side passage to the main hall, and there paused uncertainly. There were low voices from what Hilda later learned was the library, and after a moment's indecision she threw open the doors across from it into what had once been the front and back parlors of the house. Now they were united into one huge drawing-room, a Victorian room of yellow brocaded furniture, crystal chandeliers, and what looked in the semidarkness to be extremely bad oil paintings. Only one lamp was lit, but it gave Hilda a chance to see the girl clearly.

She was a lovely creature, she thought. Perhaps eighteen; it was hard to tell these days. But certainly young and certainly troubled. She closed the double doors behind her, after a hurried glance into the hall.

"I had to speak to you alone," she said breathlessly. "It's about my grandmother. Don't—please don't think she is queer, or anything like that. If she acts strangely it's because she has reason to."

Hilda felt sorry for the girl. She looked on the verge of tears. But her voice was matter-of-fact.

"I'm accustomed to old ladies who do odd things," she said, smiling. "What do you mean by a reason?"

Janice, however, did not hear her. Across the hall a door had opened, and the girl was listening. She said, "Excuse me for a minute, will you?" and darted out, closing the doors behind her. There followed a low exchange of voices in the hall. Then the doors were opened again, and a man stepped into the room. He was a big man, with a tired face and a mop of heavy dark hair, prematurely gray over the ears. Hilda felt a sudden sense of shock. It was Frank Garrison, but he was far removed from the bridegroom of almost twenty years ago. He was still handsome, but he looked his age, and more. Nevertheless, he had an attractive smile as he took her hand.

"I'm glad you're here," he said. "My daughter told me you were coming. My name is Garrison. I hope you'll see that she gets some rest, Miss Adams. She's been carrying a pretty heavy load."

"That's what I'm here for," said Hilda cheerfully.

"Thank you. I've been worried. Jan is far too thin. She doesn't get enough sleep. Her grandmother—"

He did not finish. He passed a hand over his hair, and Hilda saw that he had not only aged. He looked worn, and his suit could have stood a pressing. As if she realized this the girl slid an arm through his and held it tight. She looked up at him with soft brown eyes.

"You're not to worry, Father. I'll be all right."

"I don't like what's going on, Jan darling."

"Would you like to see Granny?"

He looked at his watch and shook his head.

"I'd better get Eileen out of here. She wanted to come, but— Give Granny my love, Jan, and get some sleep tonight."

As he opened the door Hilda saw a small blond woman in the hall. She was drawing on her gloves and gazing at the door with interest. She had a sort of faded prettiness, and a slightly petulant look. Janice seemed embarrassed.

"This is Miss Adams, Eileen," she said. "Granny is nervous, so she's going to look after her."

Eileen acknowledged Hilda with a nod, and turned to the girl.

"If you want my opinion, Jan," she said coolly, "Granny ought to be in an institution. All this stuff about bats and so on! It's ridiculous."

Janice flushed but said nothing. Frank Garrison opened the front door, his face set.

"I wish you would keep your ideas to yourself, Eileen," he said. "Let's get out of here. 'Night Jan."

With the closing of the door Hilda turned to the girl. To her surprise Jan's eyes were filled with tears.

"I'm sorry," she said, fumbling in her sleeve for a handkerchief. "I never get used to his going away like that. You know they are divorced, my father and mother. Eileen is his second wife." She wiped her eyes and put the handkerchief away.

"He can come only when Mother's out. She—they're not very friendly."

"I see," said Hilda cautiously.

"I was devoted to my father, but when the court asked me what I wanted to do, I said I would stay here. My grandmother had taken it very hard. The divorce, I mean. She loved my father. Then, too"—she hesitated—"he married Eileen very soon after, and I—well, it seemed best to stay. I thought I'd better tell you," she added. "Eileen doesn't come often, but since you've seen her—"

She broke off, and Hilda saw that she was trembling.

"See here," she said. "You're tired. Suppose you tell me all this tomorrow? Just now you need your bed and a good sleep. Why not take me up to my patient and forget about it until then?"

Janice shook her head. She was quieter now. Evidently the emotional part of her story was over.

"I'm all right," she said. "You have to know before you see my grandmother. I was telling you why I am here, wasn't I? It wasn't only because of Grandmother. My mother was terribly unhappy, too. She's never been the same since. They both seemed to need me. But of course Granny needed me most."

Hilda said nothing, but her usually bland face was stiff. The complete selfishness of the aged, she thought. This girl who should have been out in her young world of sport and pleasure, living in this mortuary of a house with two dismal women. For how long? Six or seven years, she thought.

"I see," she said dryly. "They were all right. What about you?"

"I haven't minded it. I drive out with Granny, and read to her at night. It hasn't been bad."

"What about your mother? I suppose she can read."

Janice looked shocked, then embarrassed.

"She and my grandmother haven't got along very well since the divorce. My grandmother has never quite forgiven her. I'm afraid I've given you a very bad idea of us," she went on valiantly. "Actually everything was all right until lately. My father comes in every now and then. When Mother's out, of course. And when I can I go to his house. He married my governess, so, of course, I knew her."

Hilda sensed a reserve at this point. She did what was an unusual thing for her. She reached over and patted the girl's shoulder.

"Try to forget it," she said. "I'm here, and I can read aloud. I read rather well, as a matter of fact. It's my one vanity. Also I like to drive in the afternoons. I don't get much of it."

She smiled, but the girl did not respond. Her young face was grave and intent. Hilda thought she was listening again. When the house remained quiet she looked relieved.

"I'm sorry," she said. "I guess I am tired. I've been watching my grandmother as best I could for the last month or two. I want to say this again before you see her, Miss Adams. She isn't crazy. She is as sane as I am. If anybody says anything different, don't believe it."

The hall was still empty when they started up the stairs. The girl insisted on carrying the suitcase, and Hilda looked around her curiously. She felt vaguely disappointed. The house had interested her ever since the day of the wedding so long ago. She had visualized it as it must have been then, gay with flowers and music, and filled with people. But if there had ever been any glamour it was definitely gone.

Not that it was shabby. The long main hall, with doors right and left, was well carpeted, the dark paneling was waxed, the furniture old-fashioned but handsome. Like the big drawing-room, however, it was badly lighted, and Hilda, following the young figure ahead of her, wondered if it was always like that; if Janice Garrison lived out her young life in that half-darkness.

Outside the door of a front room upstairs the girl paused. She gave a quick look at Hilda before she tapped at the door, a look that was like a warning.

"It's Jan, Granny," she said brightly. "May I come in?"

Somebody stirred in the room. There were footsteps, and then a voice.

"Are you alone, Jan?"

"I brought the nurse Doctor Brooke suggested. You'll like her, Grandmother. I do."

Very slowly a key turned in a lock. The door was opened a few inches, and a little old woman looked out. Hilda was startled. She had remembered Mrs. Fairbanks as a dominant woman, handsome in a stately way, whose visits to the hospital as a member of the board had been known to send the nurses into acute attacks of jitters. Now she was incredibly shrunken. Her eyes, however, were still bright. They rested on Hilda shrewdly. Then, as though her inspection had satisfied her, she took off what was evidently a chain and opened the door.

"I've still got it," she said triumphantly.

"That's fine. This is Miss Adams, Granny."

The old lady nodded. She did not shake hands.

"I don't want to be nursed," she said, peering up at Hilda. "I want to be watched. I want to know who is trying to scare me, and why. But I don't want anyone hanging over me. I'm not sick."

"That's all right," Hilda said. "I won't bother you."

"It's the nights." The old voice was suddenly pathetic. "I'm all right in the daytime. You can sleep then. Jan has a room for you. I want somebody by me at night. You could sit in the hall, couldn't you. Outside my door, I mean. If there's a draft, Jan can get you a screen. You won't go to sleep, will you? Jan's been doing it, but she dozes. I'm sure she dozes."

Janice looked guilty. She picked up the suitcase.

"I'll show you your room," she said to Hilda. "I suppose you'll want to change."

She did not speak again until the old lady's door had been closed and locked behind them.

"You see what I mean," she said as they went down the hall. "She's perfectly sane, and something is going on. She'll tell you about it. I don't understand it. I can't. I'm nearly crazy."

"You're nearly dead from loss of sleep," said Hilda grimly. "What is it she says she still has?"

"I'd rather she'd tell you herself, Miss Adams. You don't mind, do you?"

Hilda did not mind. Left alone, she went about her preparations with businesslike movements, unpacked her suitcase, hung up her fresh uniforms, laid out her knitting bag, her flashlight, her hypodermic case, thermometer, and various charts. After that she dressed methodically, white uniform, white rubber-soled shoes, stiff white cap. But she stood for some time, looking down at the .38-caliber automatic which still lay in the bottom of the case. It had been a gift from the inspector.

"When I send you somewhere it's because there's trouble," he had said. "Learn to use it, Hilda. You may never need it. Then again you may."

Well, she had learned to use it. She could even take it apart,

clean it, and put it together again, and once or twice just knowing she had it had been important. But now she left it locked in
the suitcase. Whatever this case promised, she thought—and it
seemed to promise quite a bit—there was no violence indicated.
She was wrong, of course, but she was definitely cheerful when,
after surveying her neat reflection in the mirror, she stopped for
a moment to survey what lay outside her window.

Her room, like Janice's behind it, faced toward the side street.
Some two hundred feet away was the old brick stable with its
white-painted cupola where Henry Fairbanks had once kept his
horses, and which was now probably used as a garage. And not
far behind it was the fence again, and the side street. A stream of
light from Joe's Market at the corner helped the street lamps to
illuminate the fringes of the property. But the house itself with-
stood these intrusions. It stood withdrawn and still, as if it resented the bourgeois life about it.

Hilda's cheerfulness suffered a setback. She picked up what
she had laid out, tucked under her arm the five-pound *Practice of Nursing*—a book which on night duty induced a gentle
somnolence which was not sleep—and went back to Janice's
door.

The girl also was standing by her window, staring out. So absorbed was she that she did not hear Hilda. She rapped twice on
the doorframe before she heard and turned, looking startled.

"Oh!" she said, flushing. "I'm sorry. Are you ready?"

Hilda surveyed the room. Janice had evidently made an attempt to make it cheerful. The old mahogany bed had a bright
patchwork quilt on it, there were yellow curtains at the window,
and a low chair by the fireplace looked as if she had upholstered
it herself in a blue-and-gray chintz. But there was little sign of

Janice's personal life, no photographs, no letters or invitations. The small desk was bare, except for a few books and a package of cigarettes.

"All ready," Hilda said composedly. "Did the doctor leave any orders?"

For some reason Janice flushed.

"No. She's not really sick. Just a sedative if she can't sleep. Her heart's weak, of course. That's why it all seems—so fiendish."

She did not explain. She led the way forward, and Hilda took her bearings carefully, as she always did in a strange house. The layout, so far as she could see, was simple. The narrow hall into which her room and Jan's opened had two rooms also on the other side. But in the front of the house the hall widened, at the top of the stairs, into a large square landing, lighted in daytime by a window over the staircase, and furnished as an informal sitting-room. Two bedrooms occupied the front corners of the house, with what had once been a third smaller room between them now apparently converted into bathrooms.

Janice explained as they went forward.

"My uncle, Carlton Fairbanks, and his wife have these rooms across from yours and mine," she said. "They're out of town just now. And Mother has the other corner in front, over the library."

Unexpectedly she yawned. Then she smiled. The smile changed her completely. She looked younger, as if she had recaptured her youth.

"You go straight to bed," Hilda said sternly.

"You'll call me if anything goes wrong?"

"Nothing will go wrong."

She watched the girl as she went back along the hall. In her short skirt and green pullover sweater she looked like a child. Hilda grunted with disapproval, put down her impedimenta—including *Practice of Nursing*—on a marble topped table, looked around for a comfortable chair in which to spend the night and saw none, and then finally rapped at her patient's door.

3.

HER FIRST real view was not prepossessing. Mrs. Fairbanks was dressed in an ancient quilted dressing-gown, and she looked less like an alert but uneasy terrier, and more like a frightened and rather dowdy old woman. Nor was her manner reassuring.

"Come in," she said shortly, "and lock the door. I have something to show you. And don't tell me it came down the chimney or through a window. The windows are barred and screened and the chimney flue is closed. Not only that. There is a wad of newspaper above the flue. I put it there myself."

Hilda stepped inside and closed the door behind her. The room was large and square. It had two windows facing the front of the house and two at the side. A large four-poster bed with a tester top occupied the wall opposite the side windows, with a door to a bathroom beside it. The other wall contained a fireplace flanked, as she discovered later, by two closets.

Save for a radio by the bed the room was probably as it had been since the old lady had come there as a bride. The heavy walnut bureau, the cane-seated rocking chair by the empty fireplace, even the faded photograph of Henry Fairbanks on the mantel, a Henry wearing a high choker collar and a heavy mustache, dated from before the turn of the century.

Mrs. Fairbanks saw her glance at it.

"I keep that there to remind myself of an early mistake," she said dryly. "And I don't want my back rubbed, young woman. What I want to know is how this got into my room."

She led the way to the bed, which had been neatly turned down for the night. On the blanket cover lay a bath towel with something undeniably alive in it. Hilda reached over and touched it.

"What is it?" she asked.

Mrs. Fairbanks jerked her hand away.

"Don't touch it," she said irritably. "I had a hard enough time catching it. What do you think it is?"

"Perhaps you'd better tell me."

"It's a bat," said the old lady. "They think I'm crazy. My own daughter thinks I'm crazy. I keep on telling them that things get into my room, but nobody believes me. Yes, Miss Adams, it's a bat."

There was hard triumph in her voice.

"Three bats, two sparrows, and a rat," she went on. "All in the last month or two. A rat!" she said scornfully. "I've lived in this house fifty years, and there has never been a rat in it."

Hilda felt uncomfortable. She did not like rats. She resisted an impulse to look at the floor.

"How do they get in?" she inquired. "After all, there must be some way."

"That's why you're here. You find that out and I'll pay you an extra week's salary. And I want that bat kept. When I saw that police officer today he said to keep anything I found, if I could get it."

"I don't take extra pay," said Hilda mildly. "What am I to do with the thing?"

"Take it back to the storeroom. The last door on the right. There's a shoe box there. Put it inside and tie it up. And don't let it get away, young woman. I want it."

Hilda picked up the towel gingerly. Under her hands something small and warm squirmed. She felt a horrible distaste for the whole business. But Mrs. Fairbanks's eyes were on her, intellectual and wary and somehow pathetic. She started on her errand, to hear the key turn behind her, and all at once she had the feeling of something sinister about the whole business—the gloomy house, the old woman locked in her room, the wretched little creature in her hands. The inspector had been right when he said it all looked damned queer to him.

The storeroom was, as Mrs. Fairbanks had said, at the back of the hall. She held her towel carefully in one hand and opened the door with the other. She had stepped inside and was feeling for the light switch when there was a sudden noise overhead. The next moment something soft and furry had landed on her shoulder and dropped with a plop to the floor.

"Oh, my God!" she said feebly.

But the rat—she was sure it was a rat—had disappeared when at last she found the light switch and turned it on. She was still shaken, however. Her hands trembled when she found the shoe box and dumped the bat into it. It lay there, stunned and helpless, and before she carried it back to the old lady she stopped at the table and cut a small air hole with her surgical scissors. But she was irritable when, after the usual unlocking, she was again admitted to the room.

"How am I to look after you," she inquired, "if you keep me locked out all the time?"

"I haven't asked you to look after me."

"But surely—"

"Listen, young woman. I want you to examine this room. Maybe you can find out how these creatures get in. If you can't, then I'll know that somebody in this house is trying to scare me to death."

"That's dreadful, Mrs. Fairbanks. You can't believe it."

"Of course it's dreadful. But not so dreadful as poison."

"Poison!"

"Poison," repeated Mrs. Fairbanks. "Ask the doctor, if you don't believe me. It was in the sugar on my tray. Arsenic."

She sat in the rocking chair by the fireplace, looking wizened but complacent. As though, having set out to startle the nurse, she had happily succeeded. She had indeed. Hilda was thoroughly startled. She stood looking down, her face set and unsmiling. Quite definitely she did not like this case. But equally definitely the old woman believed what she was saying.

"When was all this?" she asked.

"Three months ago. It was in the sugar on my breakfast tray."

"You are sure you didn't imagine it?"

"I didn't imagine that bat, did I?"

She went on. She had strawberries the morning it happened. She always had her breakfast in her room. The arsenic was in the powdered sugar, and she had almost died.

"But I didn't," she said. "I fooled them all. And I didn't imagine it. The doctor took samples of everything. It was in the sugar. That's the advantage of having a young man," she said. "This boy is smart. He knows all the new things. If I'd had old Smythe

I'd have died. Jan got young Brooke. She'd met him somewhere. And he was close. He lives across from the stable on Huston Street. It was arsenic, all right."

Hilda looked—and felt—horrified.

"What about the servants?" she said sharply.

"Had them for years. Trust them more than I trust my family."

"Who brought up the tray?"

"Janice."

"But you can't suspect her, Mrs. Fairbanks."

"I suspect everybody," said Mrs. Fairbanks grimly.

Hilda sat down. All at once the whole situation seemed incredible—the deadly quiet of the house, the barred and screened windows, the thick atmosphere of an unaired room, this talk of attempted murder, and the old woman in the rocking chair, telling calmly of an attempt to murder her.

"Of course you notified the police," she said.

"Of course I did nothing of the kind."

"But the doctor—"

Mrs. Fairbanks smiled, showing a pair of excellent dentures.

"I told him I took it myself by mistake," she said. "He didn't believe me, but what could he do? For a good many years I have kept this family out of the newspapers. We have had our troubles, like other people. My daughter's divorce, for one thing." Her face hardened. "A most tragic and unnecessary thing. It lost me Frank Garrison, the one person I trusted. And my son Carlton's unhappy marriage to a girl far beneath him. Could I tell the police that a member of my family was trying to kill me?"

"But you don't know that it is a member of your family, Mrs. Fairbanks."

"Who else? I have had my servants for years. They get a little by my will, but they don't know it. Not enough anyhow to justify their trying to kill me. Amos, my old coachman, drives my car when I go out, and I usually take Janice with me. He may not be fond of me. I don't suppose he is, but he won't let anything happen to Jan. He used to drive her around in her pony cart."

Hilda was puzzled. Mrs. Fairbank's own attitude was bewildering. It was as though she were playing a game with death, and so far had been victorious.

"Have there been any attempts since?" she asked.

"I've seen to that. When I eat downstairs I see that everybody eats what I do, and before I do. And I get my breakfasts up here. I squeeze my own orange juice, and I make my coffee in a percolator in the bathroom. And I don't take sugar in it! Now you'd better look around. I've told you what you're here for."

Hilda got up, her uniform rustling starchily. She was convinced now that something was wrong, unless Mrs. Fairbanks was not rational, and that she did not believe. There was the hard ring of truth in her voice. Of course she could check the poison story with Dr. Brooke. And there was the bat. Even supposing that the old lady was playing a game of some sort for her own purposes, how, living the life she did, could she have obtained a bat? Hilda had no idea how anyone got possession of such a creature. Now and then one saw them at night in the country. Once in her child hood one had got into the house, and they had all covered their heads for fear it would get in their hair. But here, in the city—

"Was your door open tonight?" she said.

"My door is never open."

That seemed to be that. Hilda began to search the room;

without result, however. The windows, including the bathroom, were as Mrs. Fairbanks had said both barred and screened, and the screens were screwed into place. The closets which flanked the fireplace revealed themselves as unbroken stretches of painted plaster, and gave forth the musty odor of old garments long used. Only in one was a break. In the closet nearest the door was a small safe, built in at one side, and looking modern and substantial.

As she backed out she found Mrs. Fairbanks watching her.

"What about the safe?" she asked. "Could anything be put in it, so that when you open it it could get out?"

"Nobody can open it but myself. And I don't. There is nothing in it."

But once more the crafty look was on her face, and Hilda did not believe her. When, after crawling under the bed, examining the chimney in a rain of soot and replacing the paper which closed it, and peering behind the old-fashioned bathtub, she agreed that the room was as tight as a drum, the old woman gave her a sardonic grin.

"I told that policeman that," she said. "But he as much as said I was a liar."

It was after eleven at night when at last she agreed to go to bed. She refused the sleeping tablet the doctor had left, and she did not let Hilda undress her. She sent her away rather promptly, with orders to sit outside the door and not to shut her eyes for a minute. And Hilda went, to hear the door being locked behind her, and to find that a metamorphosis had taken place in the hall outside. A large comfortable chair had been brought and placed by the table near the old lady's door. There was a reading lamp beside it, and the table itself was piled high with books and magazines. In addition there was a screen to cut off drafts, and as she looked Janice came up the front stairs carrying a heavy tray.

She was slightly breathless.

"I hope you don't mind," she said. "There's coffee in a Thermos. I had Maggie make it when I knew you were coming. Maggie's the cook. You see, Grandmother doesn't want to be left. If you went downstairs for supper—"

Hilda took the tray from her.

"I ought to scold you," she said severely. "I thought I sent you to bed."

"I know. I'm sorry. I'm going now." She looked at Hilda shyly. "I'm so glad you're here," she said. "Now nothing can happen, can it?"

Days later Hilda was to remember the girl's face, too thin but now confident and relieved, the sounds of Mrs. Fairbanks moving about in her locked room, the shoe box with the captive bat on the table, and her own confident voice.

"Of course nothing can happen. Go to bed and forget all about it."

Janice did not go at once, however. She picked up Hilda's textbook and opened it at random.

"I suppose it's pretty hard, studying to be a nurse."

"It's a good bit more than study."

"I would like to go into a hospital. But, of course, the way things are— It must be wonderful to—well, to know what a doctor means when he says things. I feel so ignorant."

Hilda looked at her. Was it a desire to escape from this house? Or was she perhaps interested in young Brooke? She thought back over the long line of interns she had known. She did not like interns. They were too cocky. They grinned at the young nurses and ignored the older ones. Once one of them had grabbed her as she came around a corner, and his face had been funny when he saw who it was. But Brooke must have interned long after she left Mount Hope Hospital.

She changed the subject.

"Tell me a little about the household," she suggested. "Your mother, your uncle and aunt live here. What about the servants?"

Jan sat down and lit a cigarette.

"There are only three in the house now," she said, "and Amos outside. There used to be more, but lately Granny—well, you know how it is. I think Granny is scared. She's cut down on them. We even save on light. Maybe you've noticed!"

She smiled and curled up in the chair, looking relaxed and comfortable.

"How long have they been here, Miss Janice?"

"Oh, please call me Jan. Everybody does. Well, William's been here thirty years. Maggie, the cook, has been here for twenty. Ida"—Jan smiled—"Ida's a newcomer. Only ten. And, of course, Amos. He lives over the stable. The others live upstairs, at the rear."

"I suppose you trust them all?"

"Absolutely."

"Any others? Any regular visitors?"

Janice looked slightly defiant.

"Only my father. Granny doesn't like callers, and Mother—well, she sees her friends outside. At the country club or at restaurants. Since the—since the trouble Granny hasn't liked her to have them here."

She put out her cigarette and got up. The box containing the bat was on the table. She looked at it.

"I suppose you'll show that to the police?" she asked.

"That seems to be your grandmother's idea."

Janice drew a long breath.

"I had to do it," she said. "I was afraid they would say she was crazy. Have her committed. I had to, Miss Adams."

"Who are 'they'?"

But Janice had already gone. She was walking down the hall toward her bedroom, and she was fumbling in her sleeve for her handkerchief.

Hilda was thoughtful after the girl had gone. She got out her knitting, but after a few minutes she put it down and opened her textbook. What she found was far from satisfactory. Arsenic was disposed of in a brief paragraph:

Many drugs, such as dilute acids, iron, arsenic, and so on, are irritating to mucous lining of the stomach and may cause pain, nausea, and vomiting. And death, she thought. Death to an old woman who, whatever her peculiarities, was helpless and pathetic.

She put the book away and picking up the chart wrote on it in her neat hand: *11:30 P.M. Patient excitable. Pulse small and rapid. Refuses to take sedative.*

She was still writing when the radio was turned on in Mrs. Fairbanks's room. It made her jump. It was loud, and it blatted on her eardrums like a thousand shrieking devils. She stood it for ten minutes. Then she banged on the door.

"Are you all right?" she shouted.

To her surprise the old lady answered at once from just inside the door.

"Of course I'm all right," she said sharply. "Mind you, stay out there. No running around the house."

Quite definitely, Hilda decided, she did not like the case. She

was accustomed to finding herself at night in unknown houses, with no knowledge of what went on within them; to being
dumped among strangers, plunged into their lives, and for a time
to live those lives with them. But quite definitely she did not like
this case, or this house.

The house was not ghostly. She did not believe in ghosts. It
was merely, as she said to herself with unusual vigor, damned
unpleasant; too dark, too queer, too detached. And the old lady
didn't need a nurse. What she needed was a keeper, or a policeman.

4.

THE RADIO went on until after midnight. Then it ceased abruptly, leaving a beating silence behind it, and in that silence Hilda suddenly heard stealthy footsteps on the stairs. She stiffened. But the figure which eventually came into view was tragic rather than alarming.

It was a woman in a black dinner dress, and she seemed shocked to see Hilda. She stood on the landing, staring.

"Has anything happened to Mother?" she half whispered.

Hilda knew her then. It was Marian Garrison, Janice's mother, but changed beyond belief. She was painfully thin and her careful makeup only accentuated the haggard lines of her face. But she still had beauty, of a sort. The fine lines of her face, the dark eyes—so like Jan's—had not altered. Given happiness, Hilda thought, she would be lovely.

She stood still, fingering the heavy rope of pearls around her neck, and Hilda saw that she was carrying her slippers in the other hand.

"It isn't—she hasn't had another—"

She seemed unable to go on, and Hilda shook her head. She picked up a pad from the table and wrote on it: *Only nervous. She caught a bat in her room tonight.*

Marian read it. Under the rouge her face lost what color it had had.

"Then it's true!" she said, still whispering. "I can't believe it."

"It's in that box."

Marian shivered.

"I never believed it," she said. "I thought she imagined it. Where on earth do they come from?" Then she apparently recognized the strangeness of Hilda in her uniform, settled outside her mother's door. "I suppose the shock—she's not really sick, is she?"

Hilda smiled.

"No. The doctor thought she needed someone for a night or two. Naturally she's nervous."

"I suppose she would be," said Marian vaguely, and after a momentary hesitation went into her own room and closed the door behind her. Hilda watched her go. She was trusting no one in the house that night, or any night. But she felt uncomfortable. So that was what divorce did to some women! Sent them home to arbitrary old mothers, made them slip in and out of their houses, lost them their looks and their health and their zest for living. She thought of Frank Garrison with his faded little blond second wife. He had not looked happy, either. And the girl Janice, torn among them all, the old woman, Marian, and her father.

The bat was moving around in the box, making small scraping noises. She cut another hole for air, and tried to look inside. But all she could see was a black mass, now inert, and she put down the box again.

She had a curious feeling that the old lady was still awake. There was no transom over the door, but she seemed still to be moving around. Once a closet door apparently creaked. Then the radio came on again, and Hilda, who abominated radio in all its forms, wondered if she was to endure it all night. She was still wondering when the door to Marian's room opened, and Marian came into the hall.

"Can't you stop it?" she asked feverishly. "It's driving me crazy."

"The door's locked."

"Well, bang on it. Do something."

"Does she always do it?"

"Not always. For the past month or two. Sometimes she goes to sleep and it goes on all night. It's sickening."

She had not bothered to put on a dressing-gown. She stood shivering in the June night, her silk nightgown outlining her thin body, with its small high breasts, and her eyes desperate.

"Sometimes I wonder if she really is—"

What she wondered was lost. From the bedroom came a thin high shriek. It dominated the radio, and was succeeded by another even louder one. Marian, panic-stricken, flung herself against the door and hammered on it.

"Mother," she called, "let me in. What is it? What's wrong?"

Abruptly the radio ceased, and Mrs. Fairbanks's thin old voice could be heard.

"There's a rat in here," she quavered.

Out of sheer relief Marian leaned against the door.

"A rat won't hurt you," she said. "Let me in. Unlock the door, Mother."

But Mrs. Fairbanks did not want to unlock the door. She did not want to get out of her bed. After she had finally turned the key she scurried back to it, and sitting upright in it surveyed them both with hard, triumphant eyes.

"He's under the bureau," she said. "I saw him. Perhaps now you'll believe me."

"Don't get excited, Mother," Marian said. "It's bad for you. If it's here we'll get William to kill it."

Mrs. Fairbanks regarded her daughter coldly.

"Maybe you know it's here," she said.

"That's idiotic, Mother. I hate the things. How could I know?"

Hilda's bland eyes watched them both, the suspicion in the old lady's face, the hurt astonishment in the daughter's. It was Marian who recovered first. She stood by the bed, looking down at her mother.

"I'll get William to kill it," she said. "Where were you, Mother, when you saw it?"

"I was in bed. Where would I be?"

"With all the lights on?"

There was a quick exchange of looks between the two, both suspicious and wary. Hilda was puzzled.

"Don't stand there like a fool," said Mrs. Fairbanks. "Get William and tell him to bring a poker."

Marian went out, closing the door behind her, and Hilda, getting down on her knees not too happily, reported that the rat was still under the bureau, and apparently also not too happy about it. She got up and beat a hasty retreat to the door, from which she inspected the room.

It was much as she had left it, except that the old lady's clothes were neatly laid on a chair. The windows were all closed, however, and the bed was hardly disturbed. It looked indeed as though she had just got into it. There was another difference, too. A card table with a padded cover had been set up in front of the empty fireplace, and on it lay a pack of cards.

The old lady was watching her.

"I lied to Marian," she said cheerfully. "I hadn't gone to bed. I was playing solitaire."

"Why shouldn't you play solitaire? Especially if you can't sleep."

"And have the doctor give me stuff to make me sleep? I need my wits, Miss Adams. Nobody is going to dope me in this house, especially at night."

The rest of the night was quiet. William, an elderly man in a worn bathrobe with "old family servant" written all over him, finally cornered the rat, dispatched it, and carried it out in a dustpan. Marian went back to her room and closed and locked the door. Janice had slept through it all, and Hilda, after an hour on her knees, discovered no holes in the floor or baseboard and finally gave up, to see Mrs. Fairbanks's eyes on her, filled with suspicion.

"Who sent you here?" she said abruptly. "How do I know you're not in with them?"

Hilda stiffened.

"You know exactly why I'm here, Mrs. Fairbanks. Inspector Fuller—"

"Does he know you?"

"Very well. I have worked for him before. But I can't help you if you keep me locked out. You will have to trust me better than that."

To her dismay the old lady began to whimper, the tearless crying of age. Her face was twisted, her chin quivered.

"I can't trust anybody," she said brokenly. "Not even my own children. Not even Carlton. My own son. My own boy."

Hilda felt a wave of pity for her.

"But he's not here tonight," she said. "He couldn't have done it. Don't you see that?"

The whimpering ceased. Mrs. Fairbanks looked up at her.

"Then it was Marian," she said. "She blames me for bringing that woman Frank married into the house. She was crazy about Frank. She still is. When that woman got him she nearly lost her mind."

"She couldn't possibly have done it," Hilda told her sharply. "Try to be reasonable, Mrs. Fairbanks. Even if she had come into this room she couldn't have brought it with her. People don't carry rats around in their pockets. Or bats, either."

It was over an hour before she could leave her. She utilized it to make a more careful examination of the room. The bathroom, which was tiled, did not connect with Marian's room, and its screen was, like the others, screwed into place. The closets revealed nothing except the safe and the rows of clothing old women collect. Hanging on the door of the one where the safe stood was a shoe bag, filled with shoes. She smiled at it, but days later she was to realize the importance of that bag; to see its place in the picture.

One thing was certain. No rat or bat could have entered the room by any normal means. The old-fashioned floor register was closed. Not entirely. There were, she saw with the aid of a match, small spaces where the iron blades beneath did not entirely meet. The grating over them, however, was tightly screwed to the floor and its openings less than a square inch in size.

Mrs. Fairbanks lay in her bed, watching her every move. She had taken out her teeth, and now she yawned, showing her pale gums.

"Now you know what I'm talking about," she said. "Put out

the light, and maybe you'd better leave the door unlocked. But don't you go away. I wake up now and then, and if I find you're not there—"

Outside in the hall Hilda's face was no longer bland. Inspector Fuller would have called it her fighting face. She waited until she heard her patient snoring. Then she tiptoed back to her room, and from what she called her emergency case she removed several things—a spool of thread, a pair of rubber gloves, and a card of thumbtacks. These she carried forward and, after a look to see that all was quiet, went to work. Near the floor she set two of the tacks, one in the doorframe and one in the door itself. She tied a piece of the black thread from one to the other and, cutting off the ends with her surgical scissors, stood up and surveyed her work. Against the dark woodwork it was invisible.

After that she put the screen around her chair so as to shield it, picked up the flashlight, the gloves, and a newspaper Janice had left for her, and very deliberately went down the stairs.

The lower floor was dark. She stopped and listened in the hall. Somewhere a clock was ticking loudly. Otherwise everything was quiet, and she made her way back to the kitchen premises without having to use her light. Here, however, she turned it on. She was in a long old-fashioned pantry, the floor covered with worn linoleum, the shelves filled with china and glassware. A glance told her that what she was looking for was not there, and she went on to the kitchen.

It was a huge bleak room, long unpainted. On one side was a coal range, long enough to feed a hotel. There was a fire going, but it had been carefully banked. Nevertheless, she took off the lids, one by one. There was nothing there, and she gave a sigh of relief. After that she inspected a small garbage can under the sink, without result.

It was in the yard outside the kitchen porch that she finally found what she was looking for. It lay on top of a barrel of ashes, and she drew on her gloves before she touched it. When she went upstairs again it was to place and lock in her suitcase the neatly wrapped body of a dead rat.

Then, having found that the door had not been opened, she calmly moved her chair against it and picking up the *Practice of Nursing* opened it at random. *The physician, the nurse, and others should report what they see, hear, smell, or feel, rather than what they deduce.* She read on, feeling pleasantly somnolent.

5.

THINGS LOOKED better the next morning. The old house in the June sunlight looked shabby but not sinister. Mrs. Fairbanks wakened early and allowed Hilda to bring her a breakfast tray. But she took her grapefruit without sugar, and insisted on opening her egg herself.

In the kitchen waiting for her tray, Hilda inspected the servants—Maggie, stout and middle-aged, over the stove, Amos outside on the porch smoking a corncob pipe, William, taciturn and elderly, and Ida, a pallid listless creature in her late thirties, drinking a cup of tea at the table. They were watching her, too, although they ignored her. She was familiar with the resentment of house servants toward all trained nurses; resentment and suspicion. But it seemed to her that these four were not only suspicious of her. They were suspicious of each other. They did not talk among themselves. Save for the clattering of Maggie's pans and stove lids the room was too quiet.

She was in the pantry when she heard William speaking.

"I tell you I put it there," he was saying. "I'm not likely to forget a thing like that."

"You'd forget your head if it wasn't fastened on." This was Maggie.

"Someone's taken it," said William stubbornly. "And don't tell me it wasn't dead. It was."

When she went back to the kitchen conversation ceased, but on the porch Amos was grinning.

Janice slept late that morning, but Marian was at the table when Hilda went down for her own breakfast. She looked as though she had not slept at all. The green housecoat she wore brought out the pallor of her skin and her thinness, and beside her Hilda looked once more like a fresh, slightly plump cherub. Marian had already eaten, but after William had served the nurse and gone, she stayed on, nervously fingering her coffee cup.

"I suppose," she said, "that Mother has been telling you how we have tried to murder her."

Hilda looked unruffled.

"I wouldn't say that, Mrs. Garrison. She did say there was an incident some time ago. Something about arsenic in the sugar."

Marian smiled grimly. She got a cigarette from a side table and lit it before she spoke.

"As it happens, that's true," she said. "That was when Doctor Brooke had the contents of her tray analyzed. It was there, all right. Only I ask you—" she smiled again, her tight-lipped smile—"would we have left it there if we had done it? Everybody handled that tray. My daughter Janice had taken it up to her. I took it out of the room. My brother Carlton carried it to the head of the back stairs and later his wife carried it down. If the servants were guilty they could have got rid of it. But nobody did." She put down her cigarette. "We may be an unpleasant family, but we are not fools, Miss Adams. We wanted to call the police, but Mother refused."

She shrugged her thin shoulders.

"What could we do? If she wanted to think we did it, that was all right with us; but life hasn't been very pleasant since."

"Was there arsenic in the house?"

"We never found any. Of course she suspects us all."

"Why should she?"

"She has the money," Marian said dryly. "She has it and she keeps it. I could leave, of course. I have my alimony." She flushed. "And I have a little place in the country. But Mother wants Janice here, and Jan thinks we ought to stay. That rat last night was merely an accident. As for the bats and all the rest of it—"

She shrugged again. Hilda's expression did not change.

"Have you thought that she might be doing some of this herself?" she inquired. "Old women do strange things sometimes. They crave attention and don't get it, so they resort to all sorts of devices."

"How could she?"

"Through one of the servants, possibly. Or, she drives out every day or so, doesn't she? She might have an arrangement—somebody handing her a package of some sort."

Marian laughed, without particular mirth.

"Such as arsenic, I suppose!"

"I gather that she didn't take enough to kill her," said Hilda dryly. "She may resent some member of the family and want to make trouble."

"She resents us all," said Marian. "All but Jan, and she uses her until I'm frantic. The child has no life of her own at all." She lit another cigarette, and Hilda saw her hands were shaking. "Don't judge us too soon," she went on. "I'd get out and take Jan, but she doesn't want to leave her grandmother. And my brother has no place to go. His business is shot to pieces. He was a broker, but that's all over. He doesn't make enough to buy shoes these days. And he has a wife to support."

She got up.

"We're not a bad lot," she said. "Even Susie has her points." She smiled thinly. "None of us would try to kill Mother, or even scare her to death. Now I suppose you'll need some sleep. I'll stay within call, if she wants anything."

Hilda, however, did not go to bed that morning. She saw that Mrs. Fairbanks was bathed and partly dressed, and made up her bed with fresh linen. Then, leaving Ida to clean the room and finish, she changed into street clothing and took a bus at the corner for police headquarters. The inspector was alone in his bare little office, and when Hilda walked in in her neat tailored suit and small hat he eyed her with appreciation.

"Hello," he said. "How's the haunted lady today?" She smiled and deposited the box and the parcel on the desk in front of him. He looked faintly alarmed.

"What's this?" he inquired. "Don't tell me you've brought me cigars."

She sat down and pulled off her gloves.

"The box," she said smugly, "contains one bat. It's alive, so don't open it while I'm here. The other is a dead rat. I got it out of a trash can, at three o'clock in the morning—if that interests you."

"Great Scott! The place sounds like Noah's ark. What do you mean, you got the rat out of a trash can?"

She told him then, sitting across the desk, her hands primly folded in her lap. She began with the arsenic in March, and went on to the events of the night before. He looked bewildered. He stared at the body of the rat, neatly wrapped in its newspaper.

"I see. And this thing couldn't get into the room, but it did. That's the idea?"

"It may not be the same one I saw in the linen closet."

"But you think it is, eh?"

"I think it is. Yes."

"What am I to do with it?" he inquired rather helplessly. "What about rats, anyhow? Don't the best houses have them?"

"They carry bubonic plague sometimes."

"Good God," said the inspector. "What did you bring it to me for?"

"I don't suppose it has any fleas on it now. It's the fleas that are dangerous. I just thought it had better be examined. Certainly somebody is trying to kill Mrs. Fairbanks."

"Just like that?"

"Just like that."

He leaned back and lit a cigarette.

"I suppose you haven't any ideas?"

She smiled faintly.

"All of them have motives. I haven't seen Carlton and Susie, the son and his wife. They're out of town. But Mrs. Fairbanks has the money and apparently holds on to it. Her ex-son-in-law, Frank Garrison, sees her now and then, but I doubt if he gains by her death. The doctor might have a reason, but she was poisoned before any of them knew him, except the granddaughter. She'd met him somewhere. He was called because he lives close by. I haven't seen him yet."

"Why the doctor?"

"I think the girl may be in love with him. And I suppose he could carry more than babies in his bag."

The inspector laughed. He had a considerable affection for her, and an even greater respect.

"You're a great girl, Hilda," he said, as she got up. "All right. Go back to your menagerie. And, for God's sake, don't get any fleas."

She took a bus back to her corner, but she did not go directly to the house. Instead she turned at Joe's Market into Huston Street and passing a row of once handsome houses, now largely given over to roomers and showing neglect, found Dr. Brooke's office in one of them. It was almost directly across from the Fairbanks stable, and a small brass plate, marked *C. A. Brooke, M.D.* and needing polishing, told her where she was.

On the steps she turned and surveyed the outlook. The stable and its cupola concealed the service wing of the house, but the rest was in full view. She could see the porte-cochere, and as far back as Jan's room. So that was why Jan had been gazing out her window the night before!

It was some time before an untidy girl answered her ring. Then she jerked the door open and stuck her head out.

"Is the doctor in?" Hilda asked.

The girl surveyed her, looking astonished.

"I'll see," she said, and ducked back.

Hilda followed her into the house. To the left was a waiting room. It was sparsely furnished with a center table, a row of chairs around the wall, and a bookcase which had seen better days. Double doors opened into the consulting room behind, where a young man, with his coat off, was sound asleep behind a desk.

The girl made a gesture.

"That's him," she said, and disappeared.

The young man opened his eyes, looked bewildered, then jumped to his feet and grabbed his coat.

"Terribly sorry," he said. "Up all night. Please come in."

He was not particularly handsome. He had, however, a nice smile and good teeth. Hilda rather hated disappointing him.

"I'm afraid I'm not a patient," she said.

"No? Well, I didn't really expect one. Sit down, anyhow. It's hot, isn't it?"

Hilda was not interested in the weather. She looked at him and said, "I'm the nurse at Mrs. Fairbanks's. I'd like to ask some questions, doctor."

She thought he stiffened. Nevertheless, he smiled.

"I can't violate any professional confidences, even to you, you know, Miss—"

"Adams is my name."

"I see. In a way I'm responsible for your being there, Miss Adams. I was worried about Jan. But I didn't expect her to get a police nurse."

"I'm not a police nurse, doctor. When there is trouble I report to the police. That's all."

"I see," he said again. "Well, Miss Adams, if you want to know whether or not I think Mrs. Fairbanks is haunted, the answer is no. She's an old woman, and she was always eccentric. Lately she has developed some fixed ideas. One is that her family is trying to do away with her. Scare her to death, as she puts it. I don't believe it. When you know them—"

"The arsenic wasn't a fixed idea, doctor."

He looked unhappy and annoyed.

"Who told you about that? The family and she herself have insisted on keeping it to themselves. I argued against it, but it was no good."

"It was arsenic, wasn't it?"

"It was. Arsenious acid. She didn't get a lot, but she got it on an empty stomach. Luckily I got there in an hour. Even at that she was in poor shape—cyanosed, pulse feeble, and so on. I washed her out, but she was pretty well collapsed."

"There was no doubt what it was?"

"No. I used Reinsch's test. She'd had it, all right."

He went on. He had wanted to call the police, but look at it! Nobody there but the family and servants who had been there a lifetime. Impossible to blame it on any of them. Impossible to have a scandal, too. And there had been no repetition. All that had happened had been a change in the old lady herself. She had been imagining things ever since. This story of things in her room, bats, rats, sparrows or what have you—

When he heard about the night before he got up and took a turn about the room.

"Well, I'll be damned," he said. "I'll be eternally everlastingly damned! Of course," he added, "things like that won't necessarily kill her. It's not murder. The other time—"

"You thought it was an attempt at murder?"

"She didn't take white arsenic for her complexion," he said grimly.

He went to the door with her, a tall, lanky young man who towered over her and who as she started out put a hand on her shoulder.

"Look here," he said. "Keep an eye on Janice, will you? She's been under a terrific strain. They're a decent lot over there, but there isn't anything to hold them together. They fight like cats and dogs. If anything happens to her—"

He did not finish.

He stood still, gazing across the street to where, beyond the fence and the brick stable, the dark rectangle of the Fairbanks house stood in all the dignity of past grandeur.

"Funny, isn't it?" he said. "When I was a kid I used to stand outside that fence to see the old lady drive out in her carriage!"

Except that she was trusting nobody just then, Hilda would have liked him that day. He had a boyish quality which appealed to her. But she hardened herself against him.

"I suppose you know," she said coolly, "that you are on the list of suspects?"

"Suspects! What on earth have I done?"

"You might have carried a few vermin into Mrs. Fairbanks's room in that bag of yours."

He looked astounded. Then he laughed, long and heartily.

"And tried to scare my best and almost only patient to death!" he said. "Come and look, Miss Adams. If ever you've seen a bag of pristine purity you'll see one now."

She did not go back, however. He showed her a break in the fence near the stable and she took that short cut to the house. Amos was washing a muddy car as she passed him, but he did not look up. He was a short, surly-looking man, and she felt that he was staring after her as she went toward the house. She had an unpleasant feeling, too, that he was grinning again, as he had grinned that morning on the kitchen porch.

She did not go to the front door; instead, she walked to the rear of the house. It was twelve o'clock by that time and the servants—with the exception of Amos—were already eating their midday dinner in a small room off the kitchen. She stopped in the doorway, and William got up.

"I was wondering," she said blandly, "whether you have a rat-trap in the house. If there are rats here—"

"There are no rats in this house," said Maggie shortly. "One was caught last night."

"You ask Amos about that. He's got them in the stable, if you ask me."

But Amos, arriving and overhearing, grouchily affirmed that there were no rats in the stable. Hilda surveyed them. They were the usual lot, she thought; loyal rather than intelligent, and just now definitely uneasy. Ida glared at Amos.

"What about that arsenic? Maybe there's arsenic in the stable."

Her voice was high and shrill. Amos glared back at her.

"You'd better keep your mouth shut, if you know what's good for you."

They were all close to hysteria, but it was left to Maggie, matter-of-fact Maggie, to put the keystone on the arch of their terror.

"If you ask me," she said, "the place is haunted. I've sat with the old lady when Ida and Miss Jan were out, and I've heard plenty."

"What have you heard?" Hilda asked.

"Raps all over the room. Queer scraping noises. And once the closet door opened. The one with the safe. I was looking right at it, and only me and Mrs. Fairbanks in the room—and her asleep."

Ida screamed, and William pounded on the table.

"Stop that kind of talk," he ordered sharply. "All old houses creak. Do you want to scare the nurse away?"

Maggie subsided, looking flushed. Ida was pale and plainly terrified. Only Amos went on eating. And Hilda, on her way upstairs, was convinced of two things, that they were all badly scared, and that they were all equally innocent.

6.

THE OLD lady's room when she reached it bore no resemblance to the eerie chamber of the night before. Someone—Jan, she thought—had been at work in it.

The sun was pouring in, there were lilacs on a table, the bed had a silk cover over it, and a number of small pillows gave it an almost frivolous look. Even Jan looked better, rested and smiling, and Mrs. Fairbanks herself, dressed now in black silk and sitting in her rocker, was a different creature from the untidy old woman of the previous evening.

Not that she was entirely changed. She was still domineering, even suspicious. Her small eyes were fixed on one of the closets, which contained the safe, and she ignored Hilda in the doorway.

"Come out of that closet, Carlton," she said. "I told you there was nothing there."

Carlton Fairbanks emerged reluctantly. He backed out, dusting his knees as he came, a small, dapper man in his forties, his thin face ruffled, his expression stubborn.

"They have to get in somehow, Mother. Why don't you let me look?"

"They're brought in," said Mrs. Fairbanks tartly.

"I've told you that. Someone in this house brings them in."

Carlton tried to smile.

"If you mean that I did it, I was out of town last night. So was Susie. Anyhow, she's afraid of rats."

"I imagine Susie has seen rats before, and plenty of them," said Mrs. Fairbanks coldly.

This for some reason caused a blank silence in the room. Carlton's mouth tightened, and Janice looked uneasy. The silence was broken only by the old lady's tardy recognition of Hilda in the doorway. She looked at her with small, malicious eyes.

"You see me surrounded by my loving family, Miss Adams," she said. "This is my son. He was out of town last night when you came. Or so he says."

Carlton stiffened. He nodded at Hilda and then confronted his mother.

"Just what do you mean by that?" he demanded. "I'm doing the best I know how. If things go on the way they are you must make some plans. As to last night—"

"I'm perfectly capable of making my own plans."

"All right. All right," he said irritably. "As to last night, if you think I need an alibi I have one. So has Susie. But the whole thing's ridiculous. Why in God's name would anybody carry these things into this room?"

"To scare me to death," said the old lady placidly. "Only I'm pretty hard to scare, Carlton. I'm pretty hard to scare."

Later Hilda tried to recall in order the events of the next few days, beginning with the lunch that followed this scene. Marian, she remembered, had been silent. In daylight she looked even more ravaged than the night before. Janice had seemed uneasy and distracted. Carlton was irritated and showed it. And Mrs.

Fairbanks, at the head of the table, watched it all, touching no food until the others had taken it, and pointedly refusing the sugar for her strawberries.

Only Carlton's wife, Susie, seemed to be herself. Hilda was to find that Susie was always herself. She was a big blond girl, and she sauntered into the room as casually as though an aged Nemesis was not fixing her with a most unpleasant eye.

"Put out that cigarette," said Mrs. Fairbanks. "I've told you again and again I won't have smoking at the table."

Susie grinned. She extinguished the cigarette on the edge of her butter dish, a gesture evidently intended to annoy the old lady, and sat down. She was heavily made up, but she was a handsome creature, and she wore a bright purple house gown which revealed a shapely body. Hilda suspected that there was little or nothing beneath it.

"Well, here's the happy family," she said ironically. "Anybody bitten anybody else while we were away?"

Janice spoke up quickly.

"Did you have a nice trip?" she asked. "Oh, I forgot. This is Miss Adams, Susie. She's taking care of Granny."

"And about time," said Susie, smiling across the table at the nurse. But Hilda was aware that Susie's sharp blue eyes were taking stock of her, appraising her. "Time you got a rest, kid. You've looked like hell lately."

She spoke as though Mrs. Fairbanks was not there, and soon Hilda was to discover that Susie practically never spoke to her mother-in-law. She spoke at her, the more annoyingly the better. She did that now.

"As to having a nice trip. No. My feet hurt, and I'll yell my head off if I have to inspect another chicken house. I'm practically covered with lice—if that's what chickens have. Anyhow, Carl can't buy a farm. What's the use?"

"Are you sure you would like a farm?" Janice persisted.

"I'd like it better than starving to death, honey. Or going on living here."

"Susie!" said Carlton. "I wish you'd control your tongue. We ought to be very grateful to be here. I'm sure Mother—"

"I'm sure Mother hates my guts," said Susie smoothly. "All right, Carl. I'll be good. What's all this about last night?"

Hilda studied them, Marian vaguely picking at what was on her plate, Janice looking anxious, Carlton scowling, Susie eating and evidently enjoying both the food and the bickering, and at the head of the table Mrs. Fairbanks stiff in her black silk and watching them all.

"I wonder, Carlton," she said coldly, "if your wife has any theories about some of the things which have been happening here?"

Carlton looked indignant. Susie, however, only looked amused.

"I might explain that I've spent the last three days alternating between chicken houses and pigpens," she said to her husband. "I rather enjoyed it. At least it was a change. I *like* pigs."

All in all it was an unpleasant meal. Yet, remembering it later, she could not believe that there had been murder in the air. Differences of all sorts, acute dislikes and resentments; even Susie— she could see Susie figuratively thumbing her nose at her mother-in-law. But she could not see her stealthily putting poison in her food. There was apparently nothing stealthy about Susie.

Marian she dismissed. She was too ineffectual, too detached, too absorbed in her own personal unhappiness. She wondered if Mrs. Fairbanks was right and Marian was still in love with Frank Garrison, and what was the story behind the divorce. But over Carlton Fairbanks she hesitated. Men did kill their mothers, she thought. Not often, but now and then. And his position in the house was unhappy enough; dependent on a suspicious old woman who was both jealous and possessive, and who loathed his wife.

He was talking now, his face slightly flushed.

"I'm not trying to force your hand, Mother," he said. "It's a good offer. I think you ought to take it. This neighborhood is gone as residential property. A good apartment building here— well, what I say is that, with war and God knows what, a farm somewhere would be an ace in the hole. We could raise enough to live on, at least."

"Don't talk nonsense. What do you know about farming?"

"I could learn. And I like the country."

There was enthusiasm in his voice. He even looked hopeful for a moment. But his mother shook her head. "This place will never be an apartment," she said, putting down her napkin. "Not so long as I am alive, anyhow," she added, and gave Susie a long, hard look.

Hilda watched her as she got up. Old she was, bitter and suspicious she might be, but there was nothing childish about her standing there, with her family about her. Even Susie, who had lit another cigarette and grinned at her mother-in-law's hard stare, rose when the others did.

Hilda slept a few hours that afternoon. The house was quiet. Susie had gone to bed with a novel. Carlton had driven out in the car Amos had washed. Marian had—not too cheerfully—offered to drive with her mother. And Hilda, looking out her window, saw Janice cross the street to the doctor's office and come out with him a few minutes later, to enter a shabby Ford and drive away.

When she had wakened and dressed she telephoned the inspector from the empty library.

"Any news?" she asked.

"I've got the report. Nothing doing. Your Noah's ark is as pure as lilies. Anything new there?"

"No. Nothing."

She hung up. There was a telephone extension in the pantry, and she did not want to commit herself. But she was uneasy. She did not think Maggie's story had been pure hysteria. She put on her hat and went across the street to a small electrical shop. There she ordered a bell and batteries, with a long cord attached and a push button. It took some time to put together, and the electrician talked as he worked.

"You come from the Fairbankses', don't you?" he said. "I saw you coming out the driveway."

"Yes. I'm looking after Mrs. Fairbanks."

He grinned up at her.

"Seen the ghost yet?"

"I don't believe in ghosts."

"You're lucky," he said. "The help over there—they're scared to death. Say all sorts of things are going on."

"They would," said Hilda shortly.

She took her package and went back to the house. It was still quiet. The door to Mrs. Fairbanks's room was open, but the closet containing the safe was locked. She shrugged and tried out her experiment. The push button she placed on the old lady's bedside table. Then she carried the battery and bell out into the hall. To her relief the door closed over the cord.

After that she made a more careful inspection of the room than she had been able to make before. She examined the walls behind the pictures, lifted as much of the rug as she could move, tested the screens and bars at the windows again, even examined the tiles in the walls of the bathroom and the baseboards everywhere. In the end she gave up. The room was as impregnable as a fortress.

She was still there when the door opened and Carlton came in. He had a highball in his hand, and his eyes were bloodshot. He seemed startled when he saw her.

"Sorry," he said, backing out. "I didn't know—I thought my mother was here."

He was looking at her suspiciously. Hilda smiled, her small demure smile.

"She hasn't come back, Mr. Fairbanks. I was installing a bell for her."

"A bell? What for?"

"So if anything bothers her in the night she can ring it. I might not hear her call. Or she might not be able to."

He had recovered, however.

"All damn nonsense, if you ask me," he said, swaying slightly. "Who would want to bother her?"

"Or want to poison her, Mr. Fairbanks?"

He colored. The veins on his forehead swelled.

"We've only got young Brooke's word for that. I don't believe it."

"He seems pretty positive."

"Sure he does," he said violently. "Look what he gets out of it!

An important patient, grateful because he saved her life! If I had my way—"

He did not finish. He turned and left her, slamming the door behind him.

Hilda went downstairs. Ida was out, and Maggie was alone in the kitchen. She was drinking a cup of tea, and she eyed Hilda without expression.

"I want to try an experiment," Hilda said. "Maybe you'll help me. It's about those raps you heard."

"What about them? I heard them, no matter who says what."

"Exactly. I'm sure you did. Only I think I know how they happened. If you'll go up to Mrs. Fairbanks's room—"

"I'm not going there alone," said Maggie stolidly. Hilda was exasperated.

"Don't be an idiot. It's broad daylight, and anything you hear I'll be doing. All I want to know is if the noise is the same."

In the end an unwilling Maggie was installed in the room, but with the door open and giving every indication of immediate flight. The house was very quiet. Only a faint rumble of the traffic on Grove Avenue penetrated its thick walls, and Hilda, making her way to the basement on rubber-heeled shoes, might have been a small and dauntless ghost herself.

She found the furnace without difficulty. She could hardly have missed it. It stood Medusa-like in the center of a large room, with its huge hot-air pipes extending in every direction. She opened the door, and reaching inside rapped the iron wall of the firebox, at first softly, then louder. After that she tried the pipes but, as they were covered with asbestos, with less hope.

There were no sounds from above, however. No Maggie shrieked. The quiet of the house was unbroken. Finally she took the poker and tapped on the furnace itself, with unexpected results. Susie's voice came from the top of the basement stairs.

"For God's sake, stop that racket Amos," she called. "Don't tell me you're building a fire in weather like this."

Hilda stood still, and after a moment Susie banged the door and went away. When at last Hilda went upstairs to Mrs. Fairbanks's room it was to find Maggie smiling dourly in the hall.

"That hammering on the furnace wouldn't fool anybody," she said. "You take it from me, miss. Those noises were in this room. And there were no bats flying around, either."

7.

THAT NIGHT, Tuesday, June the tenth, Hilda had a baffling experience of her own.

Rather to her surprise Mrs. Fairbanks had accepted the bell without protest. "Provided you keep out unless I ring it," she said. "I don't want you running in and out. Once I've settled for the night you stay out. But don't you leave that door. Not for a minute."

She was tired, however, after her drive. Hilda, taking her pulse, was not satisfied with it. She coaxed her to have her dinner in bed, and that evening she called the doctor.

"I think she's overdone, and I know she's frightened," she said. "Can you come?"

"Try to keep me away," he said. "I use the short cut. One minute and thirty seconds!"

He was highly professional, however, when he stood beside Mrs. Fairbanks's bed and smiled down at her.

"Just thought I'd look you over tonight," he said. "Can't have a nurse reporting that I neglect a patient. How's everything?"

"She's not a nurse. She's a policeman," said the old lady surprisingly. "I'm not easy to fool, doctor. That officer I talked to suggested a companion, and *she* comes. Maybe it's just as well. I don't intend to be murdered in my bed."

He pretended immense surprise.

"Well, well," he said. "A policewoman! We'll have to be careful, won't we? And I've had an eye on the spoons for weeks!"

He ordered her some digitalis and sat with her for a while. But some of his boyishness was gone. Hilda, following him out of the room as he went down the stairs, heard him speaking to Jan in the hall below. Their voices, though guarded, carried up clearly.

"We're not so smart, are we, darling?" he said. "Miss Gimlet-Eyes up there isn't missing a trick."

"I don't want her to miss anything, Court."

"Are you sure of that?"

His tone was quizzical, but there was anxiety in it too.

"Certainly I am." Jan's voice was defiant. "So are you. But if the police—"

"Look, sweet," he said. "If and when your grandmother dies, it will be a natural death. The police won't come into it at all. Only, for God's sake, don't tell the family that the Adams woman is on the watch. If there's any funny business going on—"

"You can't suspect them, Court."

"Can't I?" he said grimly. "You'd be surprised what I can suspect."

He went out the side door under the porte-cochere, his head down, his face moody and unhappy. Near the stable, however, he roused. A figure had slid stealthily into the door leading up to Amos's rooms, and he dropped his bag and plunged in after it. To his dismay it was a woman. She was cowering against the wall at the foot of the stairs and softly moaning.

He let go of her and lit a match, to find Ida gazing at him with horrified eyes. She looked ready to faint, and he caught hold of her.

"Here, here," he said, "none of that! I'm damned sorry, Ida. I didn't know it was you."

He eased her down on the steps. Her color came back slowly, although she was still breathless.

"I was scared," she said. "I saw someone coming at me in the dark, and I thought—" She stopped and picked up a parcel she had dropped. "It's my day out, sir. I was just coming home."

"Better use the driveway after this," he told her. "I'll watch you to the house."

She went on slowly, while he retrieved his bag. But his own nerves were badly shaken. He let himself into the house across the street, to find the slatternly girl in his back office avidly studying the plates in one of his medical books. He strode in and jerked the book out of her hands.

"Keep that filthy nose of yours out of my books and out of my office," he snapped. "Not that I think you have anything to learn, at that. Now get out and keep out."

The girl went out sniveling. He felt ashamed of his anger. And he was tired. He yawned. But he did not go to bed. He picked up a cap from the hall and, after a brief survey of the Fairbanks property across the street, went cautiously back there and moved toward the house.

Back at the Fairbanks house the evening was following what Hilda gathered was its usual pattern. In the small morning room behind the library Susie and Carlton bickered over a game of gin-rummy. Jan, after seeing that Hilda was fixed for the night, went to bed. And Marian, having read for an hour or two in the library, came up to bed. Apparently none of them outside of Jan suspected Hilda's dual role. But Marian paused for a time in the upper hall.

"It isn't serious, is it? Mother's heart, I mean."

"No. Her pulse was weak. It's better now."

Marian stood still, looking at her mother's door. She looked better now, dressed and made up for the evening. Jan's resemblance to her was stronger. On apparently an impulse she drew up a chair and sat down.

"I suppose she has talked about me? My divorce, I mean."

"She mentioned it. That's all."

Marian's face hardened.

"I begged her not to bring that woman here as Jan's governess," she said. "I knew her type. When she had been here a month I almost went on my knees to Mother to have her sent away. But she wouldn't. She said Jan was fond of her."

Hilda picked up her knitting. She kept her head bent over it, the picture of impersonal interest.

"All divorces are sad," she said. "Especially when there are children."

"I stood it for years. I could see her, day after day, undermining me. I wanted to go away and live somewhere else, but my— but my husband didn't want to leave Mother alone. At least that's what he said. I know better now. Carlton had got out, but I had to stay."

If anyone was to be murdered, Hilda considered, it would probably be Eileen, the second Mrs. Garrison. It was obvious that Marian was bitterly jealous of her successor. She changed the subject tactfully.

"Tell me, Mrs. Garrison," she said, "when did all this begin? I mean, the arsenic and the bats and so on."

Marian's flush subsided. She pulled herself together with an effort.

"I don't know exactly," she said. "Mother wanted a safe in her room, God knows why. It was installed while I took her to Florida in February. We got home on the ninth of March, and a day or two later she got the poison. If it was poison."

"And the bats?"

"I don't know. She didn't tell us about them at first. She said she opened the screens, and let them out. That was before she had her screens fastened. None of us believed her, I'm afraid. After all, bats and birds and rats do get into houses, don't they?"

She smiled faintly, and Hilda smiled back at her.

"I suppose the raps come under the same category," she said mildly.

Marian looked startled.

"Raps? What raps?"

"The servants say there are noises at night in your mother's room. I talked to Maggie. She doesn't strike me as a neurotic type."

But Marian only shrugged.

"Oh, Maggie!" she said. "She's at a bad time of life. She can imagine anything. And you know servants. They like to raise a fuss. Their lives are pretty drab, I imagine. Anything for excitement."

She got up and put out her cigarette. She was slightly flushed.

"We have trouble enough without inviting any, Miss Adams," she said. "I don't give the orders in this house, but I'd be glad if you didn't take the servants into your confidence."

She went on into her room, her head high and the short train of her black dress trailing behind her. Hilda, watching her, felt that something like the furies of hell were bottled up in her thin body; hatred for the woman who had supplanted her, resentment toward her mother, scorn and contempt for Susie, indignation at her brother. She put down her knitting—she loathed having to knit—and considered one by one the occupants of the house. Marian, frustrated and bitterly unhappy; Carlton, timid toward his mother, slightly pompous otherwise, certainly discontented; Susie, shrewd, indifferent, and indolent. Jan she left out, but she considered Courtney Brooke for some time.

The girl would probably be an heiress when Mrs. Fairbanks died, and he had known her before the poisoning incident. If he was earning more than his rent she would be surprised. And he had been very glib about the arsenious acid, very sure of what it was. Perhaps she had not been meant to have it at breakfast? Suppose she had had it at night, with her door locked and unable to call for help? One thing was certain. He was afraid of her, Hilda. That remark about Miss Gimlet-Eyes had left her rather annoyed. On the other hand—

By midnight the house had settled down. In his room next to his mother's Carlton was snoring comfortably. Janice was apparently asleep. From the transom over Susie's door came a light and the odor of a burning cigarette, and Marian had not reappeared. Hilda went cautiously into the old lady's room and stood listening. She was asleep, breathing quietly, but the air in the room was close and hot. Mrs. Fairbanks had refused to have a window open. She stood in the darkness, worrying. There should be air. Heart cases needed oxygen. She tiptoed to a window and suddenly stopped.

There was a sound behind her, a faint scraping sound as though something had been moved. She turned sharply, but the room was as it had been. The old lady had not stirred. Then she saw it. The door to the closet which held the safe was slowly moving. In the light from the hall it edged out six inches or more, creaking as it came.

She stared at it incredulously. Then she took a quick step forward, and as carefully as it had opened it began to close again. Not entirely. The latch did not click. But close it did, and she found herself staring at it, the very hair on her scalp lifting with horror. She did not dare give herself time to think. She walked over with buckling knees and stood outside of it.

"Come out," she said in a low voice. "Whoever is in there, come out or I'll raise an alarm."

There was no reply, and when she tried the door it swung open easily in her hand. The closet was empty. The shoebag hung undisturbed, the safe was closed, the row of dresses harbored no lurking figure. She felt deflated, as though all the breath had gone out of her. *It's a trick,* she thought furiously. *A part of the campaign to terrify the old lady. A trick! A dirty trick! And it's been tried tonight because her heart hasn't been too strong. If she had wakened and seen it—*

She hurried out into the hall. Nothing there had changed, however. Carlton was still snoring, and when she went back along the hall to Susie's open door that lady put down a magazine with a lurid cover and stared at her.

"Hello!" she said. "Anything wrong?"

Hilda studied her, the gleam of cold cream on her face, the half-smoked cigarette in her fingers.

"Somebody's playing tricks around this house," she said. "And don't tell me I imagine it, or that it's done with mirrors. It's got to stop. I've got a patient to consider."

Susie sat up in bed.

"What sort of tricks?" she inquired with interest.

"Were you in your husband's room just now, Mrs. Fairbanks?"

Susie raised her eyebrows and grinned. The connecting door into Carlton's room was open, and through it came the unmistakable snoring of a sleeping man, which begins softly and rises gradually to an ear-splitting snort.

"Listen to that," she said. "If you think Carl is in any mood for amorous dalliance—"

Hilda left her abruptly, the amused smile still on her face, and went on. Jan was in bed, sleeping like a tired child. Marian's door was locked. And there was nobody else. In a cold rage she got her gun from the suitcase and took it forward. In the same rage she folded back the screen, so that it gave her an unimpeded view of the hall. And still in the implacable anger of a woman who has been the victim of a cheap trick she crept into Mrs. Fairbanks's room and examined the closet again, this time with her flashlight. There was no break in the plaster, no place where anything could have been introduced to open the door and close it again.

She spent the remainder of the night in baffled indignation. Her patient slept. No sounds came from the door. At seven she heard the servants going down the back staircase, and shortly after Ida brought her a cup of coffee. She asked the girl to take her place for a few minutes.

"I want to go up to the third floor," she said. "I thought I heard somebody up there last night."

Ida looked surprised.

"There was nobody up there, miss. Not in the front of the house."

"Well, I'll look at it anyhow," she said, and climbed the stairs.

The upper floor was much like the second. Two large rooms across the front and a smaller one above Carlton's were evidently guest rooms. They were long unused, however. Dustcloths covered the furniture and beds, and a faint film of dust showed that rooms and baths were given only periodical cleanings. Hilda paid particular attention to the one over Mrs. Fairbanks. It had a fireplace, like the room below, but it had evidently been long unused. The dust on the hearth was undisturbed, and the flue in the chimney was closed.

There was a closet there, similar to the one below, and this she examined minutely, going over the sides and floor boards. But she discovered nothing out of the way. She thought dejectedly that she would have to come to the theory of a ghost after all.

8.

YOUNG BROOKE looked tired that morning. Jan was sleeping late, and she was still not around when he made his morning call. He stood over the old lady's bed, and protested her intention of getting up.

"You're not as young as you used to be," he said, smiling down at her. "If you won't take care of yourself we have to do it for you, Mrs. Fairbanks."

"I've got the Adams woman to do that," she retorted dryly. "I don't trust any of the rest of you. And I've noticed that she doesn't bring any bats in with her. I can't say that of anybody else."

Very gravely he offered to let her look into his bag, and the bit of foolery seemed to amuse her.

"Get on with you," she said. "If you'd wanted to kill me why would you have pumped the poison out of me?"

It was rather grisly, but she seemed to enjoy it. Outside the door, however, young Brooke lost his professional cheerfulness. He glanced about and lowered his voice.

"I wish you'd tell Jan something for me," he said. "Just tell her it's all right. She will understand."

"I'm not so sure it's all right, doctor."

Then and there she reported the incident of the closet door. He was puzzled rather than alarmed.

"Of course, a house as old as this—"

"It had nothing to do with the age of the house," she said tartly. "Something opened it and then closed it. I was there. I saw it."

He did not answer. He picked up his bag and glanced back toward Jan's room.

"Don't forget to tell her," he said. "Nobody was around the place. She's got a fool idea somebody gets in at night. Well, tell her that nobody did. Or tried to."

"You mean you watched all night?"

"You and me both, Miss Adams," he said, with a return of his old manner. "You and me both."

She had a strong feeling that she should report the door incident to the inspector. There was some sort of pernicious activity going on. When she went back to Mrs. Fairbanks's room she took the first opportunity to examine the door. It could be opened, she thought; a string tied to the knob and carried out into the hall might do it. But she could see no way by which it could be closed again.

Jan relieved her for sleep, but she did not go to bed. The June day was bright and warm, so she wandered into the grounds. Outside the garage Amos was tinkering with one of the three cars, and she wandered over in that direction.

"Good morning," she said. "I can remember this place when they kept horses."

"Pity they ever changed," said Amos grumpily.

"Mind if I look around a bit?"

He muttered something, and she went inside.

Behind the former carriage house was the tack room, and then came seven or eight fine old box stalls, now empty save for Amos's gardening implements and two or three long pieces of rubber hose.

Amos had stopped work and was watching her. She was aware of his hard, intent stare. But her eyes were fixed on the hose. A motor going in the garage at night, a long hose leading into the house, perhaps to the furnace, and Mrs. Fairbanks's windows closed. All the other windows open where people slept, but the old lady—

Amos was still watching her. She smiled at him blandly.

"Mind if I go upstairs?" she said. "I've always longed to see out of that cupola."

"I live up there."

"You don't live in the cupola, do you?"

She had a strong impression that he did not want her to go up. Then he shrugged and gave her a faint grin.

"All right," he granted. "But you won't find anything."

So Amos knew why she was there! She felt uneasy as she started up the stairs, and even more so when she discovered that he was behind her. He did not speak, however. He merely followed her. But at the top he ostentatiously reached inside for the key to the door leading to his own quarters and locked it. What was left was only the old hayloft, and over it the cupola, dusty and evidently unused for years. There was a ladder lying on the floor, but Amos made no move to lift it.

"What's up there?" she asked.

"Nothing. Used to be pigeons. I've boarded it up. None there now."

She abandoned the idea of the cupola, and took a brief look

at the loft itself. It was dark, but she could see that it was filled with cast-offs of the house itself. She could make out broken chairs, a pile of dusty books, an ancient butterfly net, a half-dozen or so battered trunks, and a table with a leg missing. Days later she was to wish that she had examined the place thoroughly that morning. But Amos was there, surly and watchful. She gave it up, and another event that afternoon drove it entirely from her mind.

Marian, looking bored, had taken her mother for a drive, and Janice after seeing them off had slipped out of the house on some mysterious errand of her own. Hilda, undressing for bed, heard her rap at the door.

"I'm going out," she said. "If they get back before I do please don't say I'm not here. I'll get in somehow."

Hilda watched from the window. The girl did not go to young Brooke's office, however. She took a bus at the corner, and Hilda finally went to bed. She slept until five o'clock. Then, having missed her luncheon, she dressed and went down the back stairs for a cup of tea, to find the kitchen in a state of excitement, Maggie flushed with anger, William on the defensive, and Ida pale but quiet.

"Why did you let her in?" Maggie was demanding.

"What else could I do?" William said. "The child brought her in and asked for her grandmother. When I said she was still out in the car she took her into the library. She looks sick."

"She has no business in this," Maggie said furiously. "After the trouble she made! She has a nerve, that's all I've got to say."

They saw Hilda then, and the three faces became impassive.

A few minutes later Hilda carried her cup of tea to the front of the house. Everything was quiet there, however, and she was puzzled. Then she saw what had happened. A woman was lying on the couch in the library. Her hat was off, lying on the floor, and her eyes were closed. But Hilda knew at once who it was.

She went in, putting down her tea, and picked up a limp hand.

"Feeling faint?" she asked.

Eileen opened her eyes and seeing who it was jerked her hand away.

"You startled me," she said. "I thought you were Jan."

Hilda inspected her. She was pale, and her lips, without lipstick, were colorless. Seen now in the strong daylight she looked faded and drab. Resentful, too. There was a tight look to her mouth.

"Jan's getting me some brandy," she said in her flat voice. "We were—we were walking near here, and all at once I felt faint. I'll get out as soon as I can. Marian would have a fit if she found me here."

She tried to sit up, but just then Jan came in, carrying a small glass of brandy and some water. She looked worried, but her small head was high and defiant.

"You're not getting out until you're able to go," she said. "Here, drink this. It will help."

Eileen drank, taking small ladylike sips, and Jan looked at Hilda.

"I'm sorry, but you'd better let me handle this," she said. "I was taking her to see Doctor Brooke, but he was out and she got faint. That's all."

Thus dismissed Hilda went up the stairs. She prayed devoutly that Eileen would be out of the house before Marian and her mother got back. But the family would have to work out its own problems. She had one of her own. If, as she now fully believed, someone was trying to get rid of Mrs. Fairbanks, either directly or by indirection, it was up to her to shut off every possible method. As she expected, the closet door was locked, and a careful examination of Carlton's behind it revealed nothing but his clothes in orderly rows and his shoes lined neatly on the floor. The register in the floor in Mrs. Fairbanks's room, however, did not close entirely. She found a screwdriver in the storeroom as well as a piece of pasteboard, and was in the act of fitting the latter into place when she heard the car drive in. After that there was a moment or two of quiet below. Then she heard Marian coming up the stairs and a moment later she slammed and locked her door.

Hilda shrugged. It was trouble, but it was not hers. She was screwing down the grille over the register when she heard Jan in the hall outside.

"I must speak to you, Mother. I must."

There was no immediate answer. Then Marian's door flew open, and her voice shook with rage when she spoke.

"How dare you, Jan? How dare you do a thing like this to me?"

"I couldn't help it, Mother. She was sick."

"Sick! I don't believe it."

"She was. Ask Miss Adams. Ask Grandmother."

"She can put anything over on your grandmother. As for you, forever hanging around her—"

"Listen, Mother. She telephoned me. She doesn't want Father to know yet, but—she's going to have a baby."

There was a brief stunned silence. Then Marian began to laugh. It was a terrifying laugh, and Hilda got quickly to her feet.

Before she reached the door, however, Marian had vanished into her room and the laughter, wild and hysterical, was still going on.

Jan was standing in the hall. She was trembling, and Hilda put an arm around her.

"Never mind," she said. "Don't worry, child. She'll get over it."

"I didn't think she'd care," said Jan blankly, and went down the stairs again.

That evening, Wednesday, June the eleventh, Marian left the house, bag and baggage. Nobody saw her go except Ida, who carried down her luggage. She left while the family was at dinner, and she told nobody where she was going. And only a few nights later her mother was murdered as she lay asleep in her bed.

9.

JAN TOOK her mother's departure very hard. She found the room empty after dinner, and Hilda, seeing her as she came out, realized that she was badly shocked.

"She's gone," she said. "Mother's gone. I don't understand. Why would she do a thing like that?"

"I wouldn't worry. She'll come back."

"You don't know her," said Jan. "She hates Eileen. She's made life pretty hard for her, and for my father, too. I'm—" She steadied herself by a chair. "I guess I'm frightened, Miss Adams."

Hilda tried to send her to bed. She refused, however. She spent the evening trying to locate Marian at the hotels in town and at the place she owned in the country. But there was no sign of her. She had not registered anywhere, and the caretaker on the small farm had had no word from her. Jan, giving up finally, looked wan and despairing.

"You don't think she would do anything dreadful?" she asked Hilda. "She's been so terribly unhappy."

"I doubt it," said Hilda briskly. "She's had a shock. She'll get over it."

The old lady took Marian's departure rather philosophically.

"What did she expect? They're married, aren't they? If they want a child—"

On the whole, Hilda thought, she was pleased rather than resentful. As though Marian was getting the punishment she deserved. But she carried through her usual routine that night, an hour or so with her door locked, the radio on, and her game of solitaire.

During that interval Hilda found Carlton in the library and told him about the night before, the noises and the moving closet door.

His reaction rather surprised her. He was alone, the evening paper on his knee but his eyes fixed on the empty fireplace. He stared at her when she had finished without replying. Then he walked to the portable bar and poured himself a drink. When he came back he looked more normal.

"I wouldn't listen to servants' gossip, Miss Adams."

"I heard the sounds myself. And I saw the door move, Mr. Fairbanks."

In the end he went upstairs to his mother's room. It was some time, however, before she admitted him. The room was as usual, the card table set out in front of the hearth and the cards lying on it, but she looked annoyed.

"Really, Carlton, at this time of night."

"It isn't late, Mother."

"It's my time for bed."

"Miss Adams heard something in here last night. I want to find out what it was."

She was quiet after that, although she watched him grimly. Reluctantly she allowed him in the closet with the safe, but he found nothing there. After that he concentrated on the fireplace. At Hilda's suggestion he tore the paper wadding out of the chimney. Nothing resulted but a shower of soot, however. No bricks were loose, and when at last he turned a grimy face to his mother it was to find her coldly indignant.

"Now that you have ruined my room perhaps you'll get out."

"If somebody is trying to scare you—"

"Who would be trying to scare me out of this house? Who wants to sell this place? Who wants to live on a farm? Not Marian. Not Janice. Certainly not the servants. Then who?"

He looked at her, soot and all, with a queer sort of dignity.

"I'm sorry, Mother," he said. "I'm trying to protect you, that's all. As to the farm, I've given that up. Don't worry about it."

He went out, carrying his coat, and Hilda watched him go. It was impossible to think of him, mild and ineffectual as he was, in connection with poison, or even with a mild form of terrorism. It was indeed impossible to think it of any of them—of Jan, young and evidently in love with Courtney Brooke; of Susie, cheerful and irresponsible; of Marian, involved in her own troubles. Even Frank Garrison and Eileen—what had they to gain by the old lady's death?

As it happened, it was Susie who told her about Frank and Eileen that same Wednesday night. Told it with considerable gusto, too, while smoking an endless chain of cigarettes. She came wandering along the hall at one in the morning, in a pale-blue negligee over a chiffon nightdress, and wearing an outrageous pair of old knitted bedroom slippers.

She pulled up a chair and took a chicken sandwich from the supper tray.

"God, how my feet hurt!" she said. "Try walking over farm fields in spike heels and see how you like it."

"I don't think I would try," said Hilda, picking up her knitting. "I have to take care of my feet."

Susie looked at Marian's door.

"Funny about her running off," she said. "Look here, you look like a regular person. What do you make of Eileen Garrison coming here today? Why did the old"—here Susie caught herself and grinned—"witch see her, anyhow?"

"I don't know the circumstances, Mrs. Fairbanks. Of course she was feeling faint."

"Yeah. She's in a chronic state of feeling faint. Can't do any housework. You ought to see the way they live!" She finished the sandwich and lit another cigarette. "Well, if you ask me it's damned queer. First Mrs. Fairbanks drives her out with curses—same like me, only I don't go. For years she doesn't speak her name or let us speak it. Then Jan brings her here and she talks to her for an hour. No wonder Marian screamed. She's still crazy about Frank. I could be myself, without half trying."

Hilda glanced at her.

"I thought you knew. Mrs. Garrison is going to have a baby."

"Oh, my God!" said Susie. "That spills it. That certainly spills it—for Marian."

It was some time before Hilda got Susie back to where she had left off. She sat grinning to herself over another sandwich until a question brought her back.

"If she was crazy about Mr. Garrison, why did she divorce him?"

Susie finished her sandwich.

"Why? Well, the Fairbankses have got their pride, or haven't you noticed? She'd caught him in Eileen's room, I guess. Maybe nothing to it, but there it was. So she goes off to Reno, and Frank, the poor sap, thinks he's got to marry the girl."

There was much more, of course. Susie, according to herself, might be from the wrong side of the tracks. She was, she said. Her father was a contractor in a small way, who liked to eat in his shirt sleeves. But Eileen was worse.

"Not her family," she said. "They're all right, I suppose. They live in the country. But they managed to get Eileen an education. However, she couldn't get a job, so she went back to the farm. And believe you me," Susie added, "there's nothing like a country girl who once gets to town. The one thing she won't do is go back to the farm. She'll grab a man if she can, and if she can't she will grab some other woman's. She tried for Carl, but I slapped her face for her. After that she let him alone. But Frank, the big softie—"

She put out her cigarette.

"I don't know just how she came in the first place. The old lady wanted a nice country girl, I guess. Anyhow, Marian was jealous of her from the start. She soft-soaped everybody. The servants liked her, and she was the nearest to a mother Jan ever had. Marian was pretty much the society girl in those days. But Eileen was on the make all the time. Well, I'd better go by-by."

She rose and stretched.

"Good heavens," she said. "I've eaten all your supper! I'll go down and get some more."

Hilda protested, but she went down, padding up the stairs a few minutes later with a laden tray. She looked indignant.

"That William ought to be fired," she said. "He left the kitchen door unlocked. I'll tell him plenty in the morning."

Hilda ate her supper, but she was uneasy. She got up and went to the window which lighted the stairs. Outside a faint illumination from the street lamps showed the trees which bordered the place, and the garage. Joe's Market on its corner was closed and dark, but there was a small light in the house where young Brooke had his office. Below her was the roof of the porte-cochere, and beyond it the vague outline of the stable.

Then she stiffened. A figure was moving stealthily from the stable toward the house. It seemed to be carrying something bulky, and whoever it was knew its way about. It kept off the driveway and on the grass, and as she watched it ducked around the rear of the building toward the service wing.

She hesitated. The thought of the huge dark rooms below was almost too much for her. But this was why she was here and, after locking Mrs. Fairbanks's door and taking the key with her, she picked up her flashlight and went swiftly back to her room. There she got the automatic and as quietly as she could made her way down the back stairs.

There was no question about it. Someone was trying the kitchen door. She did not turn on her light. She listened, and the footsteps moved on to the pantry. Here whoever it was was trying to pry up a window and—with her gun ready—she threw the light of her flashlight full in his face.

It was Carlton Fairbanks, and at first he seemed too startled for speech. Then he recovered somewhat.

"Get that damned light out of my face," he shouted furiously. "And who locked the kitchen door?"

Hilda, too, had recovered.

"Your wife found it open. If you'll go around I'll let you in. I thought you were a burglar."

She turned on the kitchen lights and admitted him. He was in a dressing-gown and slippers, and whatever he had been carrying was not in sight. His anger was gone. He looked embarrassed and uneasy, especially when he saw the automatic in her hand.

"Always carry a thing like that?"

"I got it out of my suitcase when I saw you coming from the garage."

He relaxed somewhat.

"Sorry if I scared you," he said. "I ran out of cigarettes, and I'd left some in the car. What on earth," he added suspiciously, "was my wife doing down here?"

Hilda explained. He seemed satisfied, but he did not leave her there. He watched her up the stairs and then went back, ostensibly to get some matches. Wherever they were he was a long time finding them. When he came up he said a curt good night. But he did not close his door entirely, and she sat in the hall through the rest of the night convinced that he was still awake, listening and watching her.

She reported to Inspector Fuller the next morning. He looked relieved when she laid no parcel on his desk.

"What? No livestock?"

She shook her head. She looked very pretty, he thought, but also she looked devilishly tired.

"No. No livestock. But I'm worried."

"You look it. What's going on there?"

"Everything, from a ghost that opens and closes doors to a family row. Also breaking and entering. And, of course, a love affair." She smiled faintly. "That makes it perfect, I suppose."

"Just so long as it isn't yours. I—we can't afford to lose you, you know."

He was grave enough, however, when she told her story.

"Any idea what Carlton was carrying last night?"

"No. I looked around this morning. I couldn't find anything. Whatever it was, he hid it before he came upstairs."

"Bulky, eh?"

"Maybe two feet high and a foot or so across. That's merely a guess."

"Seem heavy?"

"I don't think so, no. He's a small man. If it had been—"

"And you think it centers about the safe? Is that it?"

"She has something in it," Hilda said stubbornly. "She gets me out of the room, sets up a card table and pretends to play solitaire. I don't believe she does."

"What does she do?"

"She gets something out of the safe and looks at it. She locks me out of the room and turns on the radio. But I have pretty good ears. She goes to the closet and opens it. I can hear it creak. Then she moves back and forward, to the card table, I think. It takes about an hour."

The inspector whistled.

"Hoarded money!" he said. "That's the first time anything has made any sense. And it's the money you're to guard, not the old lady."

"It might be both," said Hilda, and got up.

He did not let her go at once, however.

"You talk about family rows, and so on. Why? I mean—why does Marian Garrison stay there? She could live on her alimony, couldn't she? She gets ten thousand a year, tax free. I've been in touch with Garrison's lawyer. Says the poor devil's business is gone—he's an architect—and it's about all he has."

"Ten thousand a year!" Hilda looked shocked.

"That's right. She takes her pound of flesh every month, and these are hard times on the alimony boys. The damned fool could probably get it reduced by court order. It seems he refuses. But if you want a motive for a murder, there it is, Miss Pinkerton. Maybe that arsenic was meant for Marian, after all."

"And the bats?"

"Oh, come, come, Hilda," he said impatiently. "Carlton wants to sell the place for an apartment. He wants to live on a farm. If he tries to scare his mother into moving, what has that to do with murder?"

"I'd like to know," said Hilda quietly, and went home.

It was that night that Susie fainted.

The day had gone much as usual. No word had come from Marian, and Jan, looking pale and tired, went with her grandmother for her drive that afternoon. On her return she came back to Hilda's room as she was getting into her uniform, but at first she had little to say. She stood gazing out the window, to where across Huston Street young Brooke had his shabby offices. When she turned, her young face looked determined.

"We must seem a queer lot to you, Miss Adams," she said. "Maybe we are. Everyone pulling in a different direction. But we're fond of one another, and we're all fond of Granny. That is, none of us would hurt her. You must believe that."

Hilda was pinning on her cap. She took a moment before she replied.

"I would certainly hope so."

"My father is devoted to her. He always was."

"So I understand," said Hilda quietly.

Jan lit a cigarette, and Hilda saw her hands were trembling. She took a puff or two before she went on.

"Then what was he doing outside our fence last night? On Huston Street? He was there. Courtney Brooke saw him."

She went on feverishly. Brooke had had a late call. When he came back he had seen a figure lurking across the way. He had gone inside and without turning on the light had watched from his window. It was Frank Garrison. His big body was unmistakable. Now and then a car had lighted it, and he had moved a bit. But he had stayed there from midnight until two o'clock in the morning. Then at last he had gone.

Hilda thought quickly. That was when Carlton had come from the stable. Had he been watching Carlton? Or had he some other reason? What on earth could take a man out of bed and put him outside the Fairbanks fence for two hours? But Jan had not finished.

"There is something else, too," she said. "Court says someone with a flashlight was in the stable loft at that same time. It might have been Amos, of course. He's a bad sleeper."

"Did you ask Amos?"

"Yes. He says nobody was there. He'd have heard whoever it was. And I've been to the loft. It's just the same as usual."

"There's probably some perfectly simple explanation for it all," Hilda said, with her mental fingers crossed. "Ask your father when you see him."

Jan looked at her wistfully.

"You don't think he wanted to see Mother? He might have thought she was out, and waited for her to come in. If Eileen told him she had been here—"

"That's something I wouldn't know about," said Hilda firmly, and went forward to her patient.

These people, she thought resentfully, with their interlocking relationships, their loves and hates, what had they to do with the safety of a little old woman, domineering but at least providing a home for them? They only cluttered up the situation. There was Carlton, annoyed with Susie about something and hardly speaking to her all day. And Marian, alone somewhere with her furious jealousy and resentment. And now Frank Garrison, probably hearing of Eileen's visit and trying to make his peace in the small hours of the night.

It was eleven o'clock that night when Susie fainted.

There had been no gin-rummy. Carlton had come up early and gone to bed. Jan had gone out with young Brooke. Even Mrs. Fairbanks had settled down early, and the quiet was broken only by Carlton's regular snoring. Hilda had picked up the *Practice of Nursing* and opened it at random.

When an emergency arises, she read, *a nurse must be able to recognize what has happened, think clearly, act promptly, know what to do and how to do it.*

That was when Susie screamed and fell. Hilda, running back, found her lying on the floor, in the doorway between her room and that of her husband. She was totally unconscious. As Hilda bent over her she heard Carlton getting out of bed.

"What is it?" he said thickly. "Who yelled?" Then he saw his wife and stared at her incredulously. "Susie!" he said. "Good God, what's happened to her?"

"She's only fainted."

"Get some water," he yelped distractedly. "Get a pillow. Get the doctor. Do something."

"Oh, for heaven's sake, keep quiet." Hilda's voice was taut. "She's all right. Keep her flat and let her alone. She's all right."

He got down on his knees, however, and tried to gather her big body to him.

"I'm sorry, old girl," he said hoarsely. "It's all right, isn't it? You know I love you. I'm crazy about you. It's all right, darling."

Susie opened her eyes. She seemed puzzled.

"What's happened to me?"

"You fainted," said Hilda practically. "You screamed and then you fainted. What scared you?"

Susie, however, had closed her eyes.

"I don't remember," she said, and shivered.

10.

Mrs. Fairbanks was murdered on Saturday night, the fourteenth of June; or rather early on Sunday morning. Marian had been gone since Wednesday evening, and no word whatever had come from her. The intervening period had been quiet. There were no alarms in the house. On Friday Hilda caught up with her sleep, and Carlton was once more the loving husband, spending long hours beside Susie's bed. He had insisted that she stay in bed.

But Susie was not talking, at least not to Hilda. She eyed her dinner tray Friday evening sulkily.

"Take that pap away and get me an honest-to-God meal," she said. "I'm not sick. Just because I banged my head—"

"What made you do it, Mrs. Fairbanks? Why did you faint?"

"Why does anybody faint?"

"I thought possibly something had frightened you. You shrieked like a fire engine."

"Did I?" said Susie. "You ought to hear me when I really let go."

But her eyes were wary, and Hilda, bringing back the piece of roast beef and so on that she had demanded, was to discover

Carlton on his hands and knees poking a golf club under her bed. He got up, looking sheepish, when Hilda came in.

"My wife thinks there is a rat in the room," he explained carefully.

"A rat!" said Susie. "I've told you over and over—"

She did not finish, and Hilda was left with the baffled feeling that the entire household had entered into a conspiracy of silence.

By Saturday, save for Marian's absence, the house had settled down to normal again. Susie was up and about. At dinner that night she persuaded Carlton to take her to the movies, and they left at eight o'clock. At eight-thirty Courtney Brooke came in, announcing to all and sundry that he had made three dollars in the office and was good for anything from a Coca-Cola to a ham on rye and a glass of beer. Mrs. Fairbanks chuckled.

"If that's the way you intend to nourish my granddaughter—" she began.

"I?" he said. "I am to nourish your granddaughter? What will you be doing while she starves to death?"

She was more cheerful than Hilda had ever seen her when at last he left her and went downstairs to where Jan waited for him in the library.

Looking back later over the evening, Hilda could find nothing significant in it. Mrs. Fairbanks had locked her door at ten o'clock and pursued her usual mysterious activities until eleven. Hilda took advantage of part of that hour of leisure and of Carlton's absence to examine both his and Susie's rooms carefully. She found nothing suspicious, however, and save for Jan's and young Brooke's voices coming faintly from below the house was quiet except for the distant rumble of thunder. It was appallingly hot, and when she was at last allowed to put Mrs. Fairbanks to bed she opened a window.

"You need the air," she said, "and I'll be just outside."

She drew a sheet over the thin old body, feeling a sense of pity for it, that age had brought it neither serenity nor beauty, nor even love.

"Sleep well," she said gently, and going out closed the door behind her.

It was a quarter after eleven when the doorbell rang, and Jan answered it. Immediately there were voices below, Jan's and another, high-pitched and hysterical. It was a moment before Hilda realized that it was Eileen's.

"So I came here, Jan. I didn't know where else to go. I can leave tomorrow," she added feverishly. "I can go back home. But tonight—"

Hilda started down the stairs. Eileen, white-faced and trembling, was in the front hall, a suitcase beside her on the floor. Jan was staring at her.

"I can't believe it," she said slowly. "Why would he leave you, Eileen?"

"He was furious because I came here the other day. He's hardly spoken to me since."

"But even then—"

"He's gone, I tell you. He packed a bag and left. He didn't even say good-by."

Jan looked bewildered. Eileen sat down on a hall chair and took off her gloves. Her hysteria was gone now. She looked stubbornly determined.

"I can't go to a hotel," she said. "I have no money. Anyhow, your grandmother told me to let her know if I was in trouble. She said that the other day. You heard her, Jan."

Hilda inspected her. She looked sick. Her color was high, and she was breathing fast. And that was the moment when Carlton and Susie arrived. They stopped and stared at the scene before them. Susie spoke first.

"What's wrong, Eileen? Frank left you for another woman?"

And then Eileen threw her bombshell.

"If you care to know," she said, "I think he's somewhere with Marian."

Jan looked suddenly young and rather sick.

"You know that's a lie, Eileen," she said, and turning went stiffly up the stairs.

After that what? Hilda tried to sort it out in her mind. Carlton went up to consult his mother, and there were loud voices from the old lady's room. Eileen leaned back in her chair, her eyes closed. Susie smoked, casually dropping her ashes into a vase on the hall table, and young Brooke came out of the library, felt Eileen's pulse, and suggested that she be put to bed as soon as possible.

"You can make other plans tomorrow, but what you need now is rest."

Her eyes opened.

"That's kind of you, whoever you are," she said faintly. "If I could have my old room for tonight—"

Unexpectedly Susie laughed.

"Not tonight, darling," she said. "Carlton sleeps there now, and Carlton sleeps alone."

After that Carlton came down the stairs. He looked irritated, but he was civil enough.

"Mother thinks you'd better stay here tonight," he said. "She suggests that you take Marian's room. It's ready. She doesn't want the servants disturbed at this hour."

Susie had giggled, but no one else smiled.

Then what? There had been the procession up the stairs, the doctor supporting Eileen, Carlton carrying her suitcase, Susie following with an amused smile on her face. Nothing unusual had happened then, certainly, unless one remembered Jan. She was waiting outside her mother's room, silent but resentful. She had switched on the lights, but that was all. The bed was not turned down.

Eileen stopped and looked at her.

"I'm sorry, Jan," she said. "I shouldn't have said what I did. I was excited."

"That's all right," Jan said awkwardly, and turning abruptly went back along the hall to her room and closed the door.

What else happened? Hilda tried to remember. Eileen unlocked her suitcase herself and got out a nightgown, but when Hilda offered to unpack for her she refused curtly.

"I'm leaving in the morning," she said. "Anyhow I hate anyone pawing over my things."

It was all over pretty quickly. Eileen settled, the doctor went back to speak to Jan. Susie went to bed, still smiling her cool smile. And going into Mrs. Fairbanks's room Hilda found her sitting up in bed, her eyes bright with excitement.

"So he's left her at last!"

"So she says."

"I hope it's true. But it wouldn't be like Frank to leave her. Now especially. Tell her I want to talk to her. I've got to get to the bottom of this."

Eileen did come, although not with any great rapidity. She sat on the side of her bed and thrust her feet into slippers, yawning widely. Then she put on a dressing-gown of Marian's from the closet and surveyed herself in the mirror.

"You needn't tell her I wore this," she said. "She'd burn it if she knew."

The idea seemed to amuse her. She tucked the gown around her—it was too long for her—and went into Mrs. Fairbanks's room. The old lady's voice was shrill.

"Come in and shut the door," she said. "Now what's all this nonsense?"

Eileen stayed for half an hour. Hilda could hear their voices, Eileen's soft, Mrs. Fairbanks's high and annoyed. And there was a brief silence, during which she heard the closet door creak. When Eileen came out she looked indignant. She closed the door and stood leaning against it.

"The old devil," she said, in a low voice. "She tried to buy me off! Look, may I have a little of that coffee? I need it."

"It will keep you awake."

"I don't expect to sleep anyhow. Not in that room."

Mrs. Fairbanks was excited when Hilda went in again, but she was certainly alive. She demanded to know why Eileen had told that cock-and-bull story about Frank being with Marian, and that she had told her she must leave in the morning. Hilda got her settled with difficulty. She was not sleepy, and she turned on the radio as the light was switched off.

"Get that woman out of the house in the morning," she said. "Get her out, or somebody will murder her."

That was at midnight. Eileen was quiet, the light out in her room. Courtney Brooke was still with Jan. Susie was reading in bed, her door open, and Carlton had gone back to the library, where he was presumably settling his nerves with the usual highballs.

At a quarter after twelve Mrs. Fairbanks turned off the radio, and soon after young Brooke, looking concerned, left Jan's room and came cautiously forward along the hall.

"She's taking this very hard," he said. "She says her father would never have left his wife, especially since she's going to have a child. She's afraid something has happened to him. I think I'll stay awhile. Where is Mr. Fairbanks?"

"He hasn't come up yet. In the library probably."

He did not go at once. He looked about him, at her tray, at the screen which shielded her from the draft, her easy chair. He thrust his hands in his pockets and took a turn or two across the hall and back.

"What about Jan's father?" he said abruptly. "Of course I know who he is. Who doesn't? Designed the courthouse, didn't he? But what sort is he? Jan's so damned loyal."

"I've only seen him for a minute or two."

"Still in love with his first wife?"

"I wouldn't know about that," Hilda said primly.

"Sort of fellow who'd get in a jam and jump out of a window? Or put a bullet through his head?"

She considered that carefully.

"I don't think so. He had a good war record, I believe. I wouldn't think he lacked courage."

"Oh, rats!" he said roughly. "It takes the hell of a nerve to kill yourself."

He went downstairs after that, his hands still in his pockets, his head bent in thought; a tall lanky worried young man, his hair on end as though he had been pushing his fingers through it. The picture, Hilda thought, of every intern she had ever known, but somehow likable. He reminded her of one in the hospital when she was a probationer. He had found her once in a linen closet and kissed her. It hadn't meant anything, of course. It had been spring, and the windows had been open. She had slapped him.

She drew a long breath and began to fill up her records.

The house was quiet after that. Below she could hear the two men's voices, faint and faraway. The radio was still at last. She looked at her watch. It was well after midnight. And then something happened which surprised and startled her.

The hall had a chandelier which was seldom used. It was an old-fashioned affair of brass and glass pendants, and now the pendants were tinkling. She looked up at them. They were moving, striking together like small bells, and she got cautiously to her feet. Someone was up there, moving stealthily about, and a moment later she had a considerable shock.

From the foot of the stairs she saw a vague figure. It disappeared almost instantly and without a sound, and when she reached the upper hall it was empty. She fumbled for a light, but she could not find it. The doors into the guest rooms were closed as usual. The long hall to the servants' quarters was a black tunnel, and at last she went down again, to find everything as she had left it. To her surprise she found that her knees were shaking. She sat down and poured herself a cup of coffee from the tray. One of the servants, she thought, curious about what was going on. Or maybe the house was haunted, after all. She remembered the opening and closing of the closet door, and found herself shaking again. Of all the absurd things! Maybe she needed glasses. But what about the chandelier?

Afterward she was to time that absence of hers; to do it with the police holding a stop watch on her. Three minutes, almost to the dot. Time to drive a knife into an old woman's thin chest, but hardly time to reach the room, commit the crime, and escape. And who could know that she would go upstairs at all? Eileen drowsy or asleep, her door closed and her light out. Susie and Jan far back along the hall, and the two men in the library below.

Yet then or later—

It was half past twelve when Eileen opened her door. She looked panicky.

"I've got a pain," she said. "Do you think anything's wrong?"

"What sort of pain?"

Eileen described it, and Hilda got up.

"The doctor's still here," she said. "I'll get him."

Eileen, however, was not listening. She was doubled over, holding herself, and Hilda put her back to bed. She lay there, softly moaning, while Hilda went downstairs. The two men were still in the library. Carlton, a highball in his hand, was looking strained, Courtney Brooke was at the telephone. He put it down when she told him about Eileen, and got briskly to his feet.

"I'd better look at her," he said. "We don't want her to abort. Not here, anyhow."

"No. For God's sake, get her out of the house before that happens. Or before Marian comes back." Carlton looked alarmed.

Eileen was watching the door as they came in. She was a pathetic figure as she lay there in her worn nightgown, her face contorted with pain.

"I'm sorry to be such a bother," she said. "I suppose it's the excitement. And my suitcase is heavy. I carried it to the bus."

He examined her briefly and straightened.

"You'll be all right. I'll give you a hypo," he said. "Do you mind boiling some water, Miss Adams?"

He followed her out into the hall. Carlton had come up the stairs. He asked briefly about Eileen and then went into his room. Hilda hesitated.

"I don't usually leave Mrs. Fairbanks alone," she said. "If I do I lock the door. But if you'll watch her—"

He grinned at her.

"Old Cerberus will have nothing on me," he said. "Do you think I want anything to happen to my best patient?"

"Something did happen. Once."

She left him with that, his bag open on the table, his hands fumbling in it for his hypodermic case and the tube of morphia sulphate. But his lightness had gone. He looked thoughtful, even grave.

Downstairs the house was dark, and the huge dingy kitchen eerie even when she had turned on the lights. It was a quarter to one, she saw by the kitchen clock. She was there for some time. The fire in the range was low, and it was perhaps fifteen minutes before she succeeded in boiling the water in a small aluminum pot and carried it up the stairs.

Courtney Brooke was where she had left him. He had poured himself a cup of coffee from her Thermos jug, and was holding it. But he was not drinking it. Some of the coffee had spilled into the saucer, and he was staring up at the landing on the third floor. He said nothing, however. He fixed the hypodermic and gave it to Eileen, still moaning in her bed.

"I don't think you'll lose your baby," he told her. "After all, it's only a month or so, isn't it? You're pretty safe. Just get some sleep. You'll be all right in a day or two."

"I can't stay here, doctor."

"You'll stay until you're able to leave."

He did not leave at once. He stood in the hall, looking uncertain and uneasy, but he merely finished his coffee. He was putting down the cup when without warning Mrs. Fairbanks's radio began to play. He started and almost dropped the cup.

"Does she do that often, at this hour?"

"She turns it on when she can't sleep. I suppose she's excited tonight."

"No good suggesting that it bothers the rest of the household, I suppose?"

"None whatsoever," she told him wryly.

He went back into Eileen's room before he left. She was still awake, but she said the pain was better. She thought she could sleep now. Hilda opened a window for her, the one over the porte-cochere, and tucked the bedclothes around her; Marian's monogrammed sheets, Marian's soft, luxurious blankets. Eileen's hand when she touched it was icy cold.

"I'll leave tomorrow," she said. "Tell them not to worry. I'll not bother them long."

Outside in the hall the radio could still be heard. Courtney Brooke picked up his bag and prepared to go. He looked young and tired.

"Tell Jan not to worry," he said. "I'll be on the job. But I'd give my neck to get her out of this madhouse."

11.

HILDA WAS quite clear as to what followed. The doctor had hardly let himself out of the house when Carlton's door banged open. He came into the hall, tying his dressing-gown around him, his hair rumpled and his face scowling.

"Good God!" he said. "Why don't you turn that thing off?"

"Your mother likes it, when she can't sleep."

"Well, she might let the rest of us have a chance," he said, and pushed savagely past her.

With the door open the noise in the hall was appalling, and he closed it all but an inch or so. He said, "Mother," but Hilda heard no reply. The radio ceased abruptly, so that the silence was almost startling. But Carlton did not come out immediately. Later she was to be queried about that.

"How long did he stay? A minute? Two minutes?"

"Not more than two, at the most."

"But more than long enough to go around the bed and shut off the radio?"

She was miserably uncomfortable.

"I don't know. I heard something creak, and I thought he had opened the door to one of the closets. His mother's safe was in it. The door always creaked."

They timed her on that, too. One of the men walked into the room, turned the radio switch and came back.

"Longer than that?"

"Yes. I'm afraid—I think it was. I know I had time to uncork the Thermos jug and pour some coffee, and I had taken a sip or two before he came out."

"How did he look?"

"I didn't really look at him. He closed the door and said his mother was asleep. He must have gone to sleep himself soon after. I could hear him snoring."

It had commenced to rain after Carlton went back to his room, a summer storm, with rolling thunder and sharp lightning. The rain was heavy. It poured down in solid sheets, and with it came gusts of wind which set the trees outside into violent motion. Somewhere, too, something was banging. Not a door. The sound was too light for that. Hilda decided to look for it and then abandoned the idea.

She ate her supper mechanically. The radio was still silent, and her watch said two o'clock when, having finished, she carried her tray to the back stairs landing to be picked up in the morning.

The sound was still going on when she went back to her post. It would stop just long enough for her to hope that it was over. Then with a fresh gust of wind it would start again.

She was listening for it when there was a crash from the back stairs, followed by a startled "Damnation" in what was unmistakably a feminine voice. When she reached the landing she opened the door to find Susie standing there, a Susie with soaking hair and in a wet raincoat over a bedraggled nightdress. She was standing on one foot and anxiously examining the other.

"Why the hell did you leave that thing there?" she demanded furiously. "I've damned near cut a toe off."

In the light from the front hall Hilda grimly surveyed her, from her sodden blond hair to her slippers, one of which she held in her hands. One of her toes was bleeding, and a cup lay shattered on the tray.

"Better let me put some iodine on that," Hilda said. "Where on earth have you been?"

"I went out to the garage. I'd left my cigarettes in the car."

"It seems to be a family habit," Hilda observed dryly. "Mr. Fairbanks did that a night or two ago. When you locked him out."

Susie fixed a pair of sharp blue eyes on her.

"Oh," she said. "So Carl said that, did he?" Suddenly she giggled. "Not very original, are we?"

She limped forward, and Hilda put her in a chair and dressed her foot, with its pink-painted toenails. But she did not go to bed at once. Nor did she produce any cigarettes. Later Hilda was to know that Susie had done a superb piece of acting that night; that she had been frightened almost out of her senses when she came racing up the stairs. Now, however, she was herself again.

She glanced at Eileen's door and laughed.

"Good heavens," she said, "when I think what would happen if Marian found her there, in her bed!"

Hilda deliberately picked up her knitting. She had an idea that camouflage was not necessary with Susie, but it did no harm to try.

"I don't suppose she would like it," she said absently, counting stitches.

"Like it! Don't underestimate our Marian, Miss Adams. She's a tigress when she's roused. She'd do anything. What on earth is that noise?"

The slapping had started again. It seemed now to come from Eileen's room, and while Susie watched her Hilda opened the door cautiously. Eileen was asleep, her face relaxed and quiet, but one of the screens, the one of the window she had opened over the roof of the porte-cochere, was unhooked. It swung out, hesitated, and then came back with a small, sharp bang. The rain was coming in, wetting the curtains, and Hilda, having hooked the screen, closed the window carefully.

Susie had not moved. She was examining her foot.

"What was it?" she inquired.

"A window screen."

"That's funny. Marian always keeps them hooked. She's afraid of burglars. That roof outside—"

She stopped suddenly, as if she had just thought of something.

"What about Eileen? Is she asleep?"

"She's had a hypodermic. She's dead to the world."

"She couldn't have opened it herself?"

"Not for the last hour or so. Anyhow, why would she?"

But the open screen worried her. She took her flashlight and went back into Eileen's room. It was as she had left it, Eileen's suitcase on the floor, the window closed, and Eileen still sleeping. She went to the window and examined the screen. It could have been unhooked from the outside. A knife blade could have done it. But if there had been any marks on the roof beneath, the rain had washed them away. One thing struck her as curious, however. A thin light piece of rope was hanging down from one of the old-fashioned outside shutters. It swayed in the wind and one end of it now and then slapped against the window itself. But although it seemed to serve no useful purpose, it might have been there for years.

She left the window and opened the bathroom door. The bathroom was empty, and so, too, was Marian's closet, save for the row of garments hanging there. When she went back into the hall Susie was still there.

"Find anything?"

"No. How long has that rope been fastened to the shutter over the porte-cochere?"

"Rope?" said Susie blankly. "What rope?"

Hilda was worried. Useless to tell herself that nobody could have entered Mrs. Fairbanks's room that night. Useless to recall all the precautions she had taken. Her bland cherubic face was gone now. Instead she looked like an uneasy terrier.

"I'm going in to see Mrs. Fairbanks," she said. "She can't do any more than take my head off."

She opened the door and went in. The room was cool and dark, but outside the wind had veered and the curtains were blowing out into the room. She put down the window and then turned and looked at the bed. She only remembered dimly afterward that Susie was standing in the doorway; that there was a brilliant flash of lightning, and that all at once Susie was pointing at the bed and screaming. Loud piercing shrieks that could be heard all over the house.

She herself was only conscious of the small old figure on the bed, with the handle of a common kitchen knife sticking up from the thin chest.

Carlton was the first to arrive. He bolted out of his room in pajamas, and stopped Susie by the simple expedient of holding his hand over her mouth.

"Shut up," he said roughly. "Have you gone crazy? What's the matter?"

Susie stopped yelling. She began to cry instead, and he looked helplessly at Hilda, standing rigid at the foot of the bed.

"I'm sorry, Mr. Fairbanks," she said. "Your mother—"

"What's happened to her?"

"I'm afraid," she said, her voice sounding far away in her own ears. "I'm afraid she's been killed."

He shoved Susie aside, switched on the lights and went into the room. He did not say anything. He stood looking down at the bed, like a man paralyzed with horror. Not until he heard Jan's voice outside did he move.

"Don't let her in," he said thickly. "Keep everybody out. Get the police." And then suddenly: "Mother, *Mother!*"

He went down on his knees beside her bed and buried his face in the bed.

When he got up he was quieter. He looked what he was, an insignificant little man, looking shrunken in his pajamas, but capable, too, of dignity.

"I'd better look after my wife," he said. "She has had a shock. Will you—do you mind calling the police? And the doctor? Although I suppose—"

He did not finish. He went out into the hall, leaving Hilda in the room alone.

She did not go downstairs at once. She went to the bed and touched the thin old arm and hand. They were already cool. An hour, she thought. Maybe more. She had sat outside and eaten her supper, and already death had been in this room, in this body.

Automatically she looked at her wrist watch. It showed a quarter after two. Then her eyes, still dazed, surveyed the room. Nothing was changed. The card table and rocking chair were by the empty hearth. The door to the closet with the safe was open only an inch or two, and when she went to it, being careful not to touch the knob, the safe itself was closed. Nothing had disturbed the window screens. They were fastened tight. And yet, into this closed and guarded room, someone had entered that night and murdered the old woman.

She was very pale when she went out into the hall. The household was still gathering. William and Maggie in hastily donned clothing were coming along the back hall. Ida was halfway down the stairs to the third floor, clutching the banisters and staring, her mouth open. Jan was standing in a dressing-gown over her nightdress, her eyes wide and horrified, and Susie was in a chair, with Carlton beside her and tears rolling down her cheeks.

Hilda surveyed them. Then she closed the door behind her and turning the key in the lock, took it out.

"I'm sorry," she said. "Nobody is to go in until the police get here. I'll call them now."

But she did not call them at once. Eileen, roused from her drugged sleep, had opened her door. She stood there swaying, one hand against the frame.

"What is it?" she said dazedly. "Has something happened?"

It was Carlton who answered, looking at her without feeling, as if he could no longer feel anything, pity or love or even anger.

"Mother is dead," he said. "She has been murdered."

Eileen stood very still, as if her reactions were dulled by the drug she had had. She did not look at Carlton. It was as though she saw none of them. Then her hold on the door relaxed and she slid in a dead faint to the floor.

12.

Hilda left her there with Jan and Ida bending over her. She felt very tired. For the first time in her sturdy self-reliant life she felt inadequate and useless. She had failed. They had trusted her and she had failed. Jan's shocked face, Carlton's dazed one, Susie's tears, even Eileen's fainting showed how terribly she had failed.

And it was too late to do anything. What use to call the doctor? Any doctor. Or even the police. The best they could do would be to exact justice. They could not bring back to life a little old lady who, whatever her faults, should not be lying upstairs with a kitchen knife in her heart.

She sat down wearily at the library desk and picked up the telephone. Even here things were wrong. It was some time before she got young Brooke's office. Then the girl she had seen there answered it indignantly.

"Give a person time to get some clothes on," she snapped. "What is it?"

"I want the doctor."

"You can't have him. He's out."

Eventually she learned that a woman had been knocked down at the corner by a bus, and Dr. Brooke had gone with her to a hospital. The girl did not know what hospital.

"Tell him when he comes back," Hilda said sharply, "that old Mrs. Fairbanks has been killed, and to come over at once."

"Jesus," said the girl. "There goes the rent."

Hilda hung up, feeling sick.

After that she called Inspector Fuller at his house. Her hands had stopped shaking by that time, but there was still a quaver in her voice. To her relief he answered at once.

"Yes?"

"This is Hilda Adams, Inspector."

"Hello, Pink. What's wrong? Don't tell me you've found some goldfish!"

Hilda swallowed.

"Mrs. Fairbanks is dead," she said. "She's been stabbed with a knife. It couldn't have happened, but it did."

His voice changed. There was no reproach in it, but it was cold and businesslike.

"Pull yourself together, Hilda. Lock the room, and hold everything until I get there. Keep the family out."

"I've done that. I—"

But he had already hung up.

She went slowly up the stairs. Ida and Maggie had got Eileen into bed and were standing over her, the door to the room open. In the hall the group remained unchanged, save that Carlton was sitting down, his head in his hands.

"I've got the police," she said. "The doctor's out. If you'd like me to call another one—"

Carlton looked up.

"What's the good of a doctor?" he said. "She's gone, isn't she? And I want that key, Miss Adams. You're not on this case now. She's my mother, and she's alone. I'm going in to stay with her."

He got up, looking determined, and held out his hand.

"No one is to go in there," Hilda said. "Inspector Fuller said—"

"To hell with Inspector Fuller."

It might have been ugly. He was advancing on her when a siren wailed as a radio car turned into the driveway. Susie spoke then.

"Don't make a fool of yourself, Carl. That's the police."

William went down the stairs. He looked old and stooped, and his shabby bathrobe dragged about his bare ankles. When he came back two young officers in uniform were at his heels. They looked around, saw Eileen in her bed, and started for the room. Hilda stopped them.

"Not there," she said. "In here. The door's locked."

She gave them the key, and they unlocked it and went in, to come out almost immediately. One of them stayed outside the door, surveying the group in the hall with an impassive face. The other went down to the telephone. With his departure everything became static, frozen into immobility. Then Jan moved.

"I can't bear it," she said brokenly. "Why would anybody do that to her? She was old. She never hurt anyone. She—"

She began to cry, leaning against the screen and sobbing brokenheartedly, and with the sound the frozen silence ended. There was small but definite movement. Carlton lifted his head, showing a white face and blank eyes. Susie felt in her draggled dressing-gown for a cigarette and then thought better of it. And Hilda pulled herself together and went in to look at Eileen. She was conscious, but her pulse was thin and irregular, and Hilda mixed some aromatic ammonia with water and gave it to her.

"Let me out of here," she gasped. "I'm all right. I want to go home."

"Better wait until morning, Mrs. Garrison. You've had a shock. And anyhow you oughtn't to move about. You know that."

Eileen's eyes were wild. They moved from Maggie and Ida back to Hilda.

"I'm frightened," she gasped. "You can slip me out somehow." She tried to sit up in the bed, but Hilda held her down.

"I'm afraid that's impossible," she told her. "The police are here. They may want to talk to you."

"But I don't know anything about it," Eileen gasped. "I've been dead to the world. You know that."

"Of course I know it," Hilda said gently. "They'll not bother you much. I'll tell them."

Eileen relaxed. She lay back against her pillows, her eyes open but the pupils sharply contracted from the morphia.

"How was she killed?" she asked.

"Never mind about that. Try to be quiet."

The second policeman had come up the stairs, and from far away came the sound of another siren. Hilda walked to the window over the porte-cochere and looked out. The rain had almost ceased. It was dripping from the roof overhead, but the wind had dropped. The room was hot and moist. She raised the window and stood staring outside.

The screen she had fastened was open again. It hung loosely on its hinges, moving a little in the light breeze, but no longer banging.

She did not fasten it. She went back to the bed, where Eileen lay with her eyes closed, relaxed and half asleep.

"I'm sorry to bother you, Mrs. Garrison," she said. "Did you open a window tonight? Or a screen?"

"What screen?" said Eileen drowsily. "I didn't open anything."

Ida got up. She had been sitting by the bed.

"Better let her sleep if she can, miss," she said. "Why would she open a screen?"

All at once the hall outside was filled with men, some of them in uniform. They came up the stairs quietly but inevitably, carrying the implements of their grisly trade, the cameramen, the fingerprint detail, the detectives in soft hats and with hard, shrewd eyes. A brisk young lieutenant was apparently in charge.

He nodded to Carlton.

"Bad business, sir," he said. "Sorry. Can you get these people downstairs? In one room, if that's convenient."

Carlton looked overwhelmed at the crowd.

"We'd like to get some clothes on," he said.

"Not yet, if you don't mind. The inspector will be here any time now. He'll want to see you all."

They shuffled down, accompanied by an officer, the three servants, Susie, Jan, and Carlton. Only Eileen remained, and Hilda, standing in her doorway. The lieutenant looked at her, at her uniform and at the room beyond her.

"Who is in there?"

"Mrs. Garrison. She can't be moved. I'm looking after her."

He nodded, and with a gesture to two of the detectives, went into the dead woman's room and closed the door. The others stood around, waiting. A cameraman lit a cigarette and put it out. One or two yawned. Hilda closed the door into Eileen's room and stood against it, but they showed no interest in her. Not at least until the inspector came up the stairs.

He took one look at her and turned to the uniformed man who had come with him.

"See if there's any brandy in the house," he said. "Sit down, Hilda. Bring a chair, somebody."

They looked at her then. The hall was filled with men staring at her. Their faces were blurred. She had felt this way her first day in the operating room. White masks staring at her, and someone saying, "Catch that probationer. She's going to faint." She roused herself with an effort, forcing her eyes to focus.

"I'm not going to faint," she said stubbornly.

"You're giving a darned good imitation, then," he said. "Sit down. Don't be a little fool. I need you."

The brandy helped her. When she could focus her eyes she found the inspector gone. But the phalanx of men was still in the hall, watching her with interest. She got up unsteadily and went into Eileen's room. To her surprise Eileen was up. She was trying to get into her clothes, and the face she turned on Hilda was colorless and desperate.

"I've got to go," she said. "If Frank goes home and finds I'm gone—I must have been out of my mind to come here."

"I can telephone, if you like. You can't leave, of course. They won't allow anyone to leave the house."

"You mean—we're prisoners?"

Hilda's nerves suddenly snapped.

"Listen," she said. "There's been a murder in this house. Of course you're not a prisoner. But you're getting back into that bed and staying there if I have to put a policeman on your chest."

That was the situation when there was a rap at the door. The inspector wanted her, and Hilda went out.

In the old lady's room nothing had yet been disturbed. Only

the detectives were standing there, touching nothing. The inspector nodded at her.

"All right," he said. "Now look at this room. You know how you left it when Mrs. Fairbanks went to bed. Is anything changed? Has anything been moved? Take your time. There's no hurry."

She gazed around her. Everything was different, yet everything was the same. She shook her head.

"Try again," he insisted. "Anything moved on the table? Anything different about the curtains?"

She looked again, keeping her eyes from the quiet figure on the bed.

"I think Mrs. Fairbanks left that closet door closed," she said finally.

"You're not sure?"

"I'm sure she closed it. She always did. But there's a small safe in it. I think Mrs. Fairbanks opened it at night. I don't know why."

"A safe?"

He took out a handkerchief and pulled the door open. He examined the safe, but it was closed and locked.

"Anyone else in the house have access to it?"

"I don't think so. She was rather queer about it. She didn't really like anybody to go into the closet, and she locked it when she went out."

"I suppose this is the closet where—"

"Yes."

He showed her the knife, still in the dead woman's chest. She forced herself to look at it, but she was trembling.

"Ever seen it before?"

"I may. I wouldn't know. It looks like a common kitchen knife."

"There wasn't such a knife upstairs, for instance? Lying about."

She shook her head, and he let her go, saying he would talk to her later. As she went out the men in the hall crowded in, to take their pictures, to dust the furniture and the knife for prints, to violate—she thought miserably—the privacy of fifty years of living. And why? Who in this house would have killed an old woman? No one seeing the household that night could doubt that they were shocked, if not grieved. And who else could have done it?

Her mind was clearer now. The radio had been turned on before young Brooke left, so she was alive then. Who else? Carlton? He had gone in and shut off the machine. He could have carried the knife in his dressing-gown pocket. But—unless he was a great actor—he was almost broken by his mother's death. He had gone down on his knees by the bed. He—

Who else? Marian was away. Jan was out of the question. Eileen was sick and under the influence of the hypodermic. Susie? But how could Susie get into the room? How could anyone get into the room?

She went back carefully over the night. Eileen had left Mrs. Fairbanks at midnight and Hilda had put her to bed. At a quarter after twelve she had shut off her radio and apparently gone to sleep. It was almost half past twelve when Courtney Brooke had gone down to have a drink with Carlton in the library, and soon after that Eileen had complained of pain.

During all that time she—Hilda—had left the door unguarded only for the brief excursion to the head of the stairs to the third floor, along the back hall to carry her tray back, and much later when Susie crashed into it. True, she had been in the kitchen for some time, but Mrs. Fairbanks had been alive after that. Witness the radio.

Her mind was whirling. She had been in Eileen's room once or twice, but only for a matter of seconds. In any case she could have seen Mrs. Fairbanks's door, and any movement outside. Susie? But the old lady had been dead for some time before she left her in the hall to close Eileen's screen. An hour at least; maybe more.

She leaned her head back in her chair. On the table still lay her equipment for the night, the heavy textbook, her knitting bag, the thermometer in its case, the flashlight, her charts and records. She could see the last thing she had written, after Eileen's visit. *Patient nervous. Not sleepy. Refuses sedative.* She felt sick again.

From beyond the closed door came the muffled sounds of men moving about, and the soft *plop* of the cameramen's flash bulbs. A car drove in below, a bell rang, and a man with a bag came up the stairs. The medical examiner, she knew. But what could he find? A little old lady on her back, with her arms outstretched and a knife in her heart.

He was a brisk, youngish man with a mustache, and he was in a bad humor when the inspector came out to meet him.

"Pity you fellows can't move without a panzer division," he said. "I had the devil of a time getting my car in."

"Well, we won't keep you long," said the inspector. "Stab wound in the chest. That's all."

"How do you know that's all?"

"It seems to have been enough."

The medical examiner ignored Hilda. He went inside the room, followed by the inspector, and was there five minutes. He was still brisk when he came out, but his irritation was gone. He seemed depressed.

"So that's the end of old Eliza Fairbanks," he said, tugging at his mustache. "Who did it? You can bet your bottom dollar she didn't do it herself."

"No," said the inspector. "No, I don't think so. How long ago, do you think?"

The medical examiner looked at his watch.

"It's half past three now," he said. "I'd say two hours ago. Maybe more. Say between one and two o'clock, at a guess. Nearer one, perhaps, from the body temperature. Hard to tell, of course. *Rigor* sets in earlier in warm weather. I'll know better after the autopsy. What time did she eat last?"

He looked at Hilda.

"She had a tray at seven-thirty," she said. "She didn't go down to dinner. Poached eggs, a green salad, and some fruit. She was alive a little after one o'clock."

"How do you know that?" he asked sharply. "See her?"

"No. She turned on her radio."

He was still brisk as he went down the stairs. This was his job. When he went to bed he left his clothing ready to put on, the cuff links in his shirt, his shoes and socks beside the bed, his tie on the dresser. Even his car had a permit to stand out on the street all night. He lived like a fireman, he would say. But now he was slightly shocked. Mostly his work took him to the slums.

Now there was a murder in the Fairbanks house. Somebody had jabbed a knife into old Eliza. Well, he'd be damned. He'd be doubly damned.

The inspector watched him down the stairs. Then he got a straight chair and sat down, confronting Hilda. There was no softness in his face. He looked angry and hard. Hard as nails.

"All right," he said. "Now let's have it. And it had better be good. No use saying it couldn't happen. It has."

She braced herself. She had failed, and he knew it. He wanted no excuses. He wanted the story, and she gave it as coherently as her tired mind would allow; Eileen's arrival, her story and subsequent collapse; Mrs. Fairbanks's demand to see her, and after that the unusual settling her for the night. Then came Eileen's pain, the two trips downstairs, one to speak to the doctor, the other to boil some water, leaving the doctor on guard, and the later discovery of Eileen's open screen slapping in the wind. But it was over Susie's appearance, wet and bedraggled, that he spent the most time.

"What about this Susie?" he asked. "Devoted to the old lady and all that?"

In spite of herself Hilda smiled.

"Not very. Mrs. Fairbanks disliked her, and Susie—well, I thought she tried to annoy her mother-in-law. But that's as far as it went."

"What about this excursion of hers? For cigarettes in the rain? Do you believe it?"

"It might have been. She smokes a good bit."

"But you don't think so?"

"I don't know. I don't think she's particularly scrupulous. But

I doubt if she would kill anybody. She and her husband wanted to leave here and buy a farm. Mrs. Fairbanks objected. Still that's hardly a reason—"

"Any chance she could have unhooked this screen over the porte-cochère? Earlier in the night?"

"She didn't come upstairs after dinner. She and Mr. Fairbanks went to the movies."

"What about later? After the Garrison woman came?"

"She wasn't in the room at all. She hates Eileen Garrison like poison."

"What's she like? Strong? Muscular?"

"She looks pretty strong. She's a big woman."

He looked back along the hall. The screen which usually protected Hilda's chair had been folded against the wall, and he had an uninterrupted view.

"Where is her room?"

Hilda told him, and he went back and inspected it, including the door to the service staircase.

"You didn't see her leave?"

"No. The screen was in the way."

"So," he said thoughtfully, "she was outside for nobody knows how long. She's big enough to handle a ladder, and she had no reason for loving her mother-in-law. People have gone to the chair for less!"

All at once Hilda found herself defending Susie. She was too direct, too open. She was—well, she was simply Susie.

"Suppose she did get into Eileen's room? Eileen Garrison was there. She was awake until she had the hypodermic. And after that how could she get into Mrs. Fairbanks's room? I was here, in this chair. When we found the body at half past two it was already—cool."

Nevertheless, he sent an officer to locate a ladder, in the house or on the grounds, preferably wet. He did not sit down again after that. He stood still, frowning thoughtfully.

"What about this radio?" he asked abruptly. "Sure the old lady turned it on herself? Somebody might have used one of these remote control affairs. They operate as far as sixty feet."

"Don't they have cables, or something of the sort?"

"Not the new ones."

The men were coming out now. He let some of them go and detained two of the detectives.

"I want every room in the house searched," he told them. "Look for one of those remote radio controls. Look for a phonograph, too. And for anything suspicious, of course. Miss Adams will have to go into the room here in front. There's a sick woman there."

They moved off, quiet and businesslike. From the driveway below came the sounds of cars starting as the fingerprint and cameramen departed. No voices came from the library, and Hilda could imagine the group huddled there, stricken and dazed. She got up.

"Now?"

"If you please."

She went into Eileen's room. Eileen was asleep, but she roused at Hilda's entrance.

"What is it?" she said peevishly.

"I'm sorry. I'll have to search the room. All the house is being searched. I won't bother you."

"Go ahead. What are they looking for? Another knife?"

But the net result was nothing. The suitcase revealed a dress or two and some undergarments, most of them showing considerable wear. The closet, hung with Marian's luxurious wardrobe, provided a bitter contrast, but that was all. And Eileen, yawning, looked bored and indifferent.

"I wish you'd get out and let me sleep."

"How do you feel?"

"How do you expect me to feel?"

She was half asleep when Hilda left the room.

The search was still going on when she closed the door behind her. One of the detectives was on his way to the third floor, and she gathered nothing had been found. There was a uniformed guard outside Mrs. Fairbanks's door, and two men in white were inside by the bed with a long wicker basket.

So Eliza Fairbanks was leaving the home to which she had come as a bride, going in a basket, without the panoply of flowers and soft music, without even dignity or any overwhelming grief.

Standing in the hall Hilda swore a small and very private oath; to help the police to revenge this murder, and to send whoever had done it to death. "So help me God."

13.

THE FAMILY and servants were still in the library when she went downstairs. They paid no attention to her. It was as though the knife, now wrapped in cellophane and in the inspector's pocket, had cut them all away from their normal roots, their decent quiet habits of living. Only Jan looked up when Hilda entered, her eyes swollen, and clutching a moist handkerchief in her hand.

"Are they through?"

"Not quite."

"But this is dreadful. We're not prisoners. None of us would have hurt Granny."

"I don't see how it's possible for anyone to have done it."

Carlton turned his head and looked at her with blood-shot eyes. He was holding a highball, and it was evidently not his first.

"Where were you?" he demanded. "I thought your job was to protect her. What do we know about you? How do we know you didn't do it yourself?"

"Oh, shut up, Carl," Susie said wearily. "Why would she?"

Watch them all, the inspector had said. *They'll have the gloves off now. Watch Carlton. Watch his wife. Watch the servants, too. They may know something. Tell them about the ladder and the screen. That may make them sit up.*

She sat down. The servants were huddled in a corner, Maggie stiff and resentful, Ida staring at nothing, her hands folded in her lap, and William on the edge of a chair, his head shaking with an old man's palsy.

"Someone may have got in from outside," she said. "Mrs. Garrison's screen was open. They're looking now for a ladder."

She thought Carlton relaxed at that. He even took a sip of his drink.

"Plenty of ladders about," he said. "Police have some sense, after all."

Only Jan showed a sharp reaction. She sat up and stared at Hilda wildly.

"That's absurd," she said. "Who would want to do such a thing? And even if they did they couldn't get into Granny's room. Miss Adams was always in the hall."

Hilda watched her. She was not only terrified. She knew something. And Susie was watching her, too.

"Don't take it too hard, Jan," she drawled. "They've got to try everything. No use getting hysterical. That won't help."

It sounded like a warning. Again Hilda wondered if there was a conspiracy among them, a conspiracy of silence. As if, whatever had once divided them, they were now united. She got no further, however. Outside an ambulance drove away, and immediately after the inspector appeared at the door.

"I'd like to talk to you," he said to the room in general. "There are some things to be cleared up. If there's a place where I can see everybody, one at a time—"

Carlton got up. His truculence had returned, and he was feeling the whisky.

"I'd better tell you," he said thickly. "I suppose this Adams woman has already done it. I was in my mother's room tonight. I went in to turn off the radio. But I didn't touch her. I thought she was asleep. I—"

"We'll talk about that later. You're Mr. Fairbanks, I suppose?"

"Yes."

"And don't be a fool," said Susie unexpectedly. "He didn't kill her. He was fond of her, God knows why. Anyhow he hasn't got the guts for murder. Look at him!"

Her tone was half contemptuous, half fiercely protective. The inspector ignored her.

"If there is a room I'll talk to you there, Mr. Fairbanks. And I'll ask you to come along, Miss Adams, to check certain facts."

"I'm not talking before her," Carlton snapped.

"Miss Adams is one of my most able assistants, Mr. Fairbanks. If you prefer to go to my office—"

But the fight was out of Carlton. He looked at Hilda and shrugged.

"All right. God knows I have no secrets. Come in here."

He led the way to the small morning room behind the library, and the inspector closed the door.

Yet Carlton's story, as it was dug out of him, offered little or nothing new. He had been in bed when his mother's radio went on. It was very loud. It wakened him. He had gone in and shut it off. The room was dark. He had seen only her outline, but she had not moved.

"You came out immediately?"

"I did."

"Are you sure of that? Didn't you open a closet door while you were in the room?"

The question took him by surprise. He looked uncomfortable.

"I closed it," he said. "It was standing open."

"Wasn't that rather curious? I mean, why do a thing like that?"

"My mother liked it closed. Her safe was there."

"Did you stop to examine the safe?"

He hesitated.

"Well, I took a look." He glanced at Hilda. "I didn't know anything about Miss Adams. I just wondered—" He tried to smile and failed. "My mother was rather peculiar in some ways," he said. "I've never seen inside the safe. But if she had money there—"

His voice trailed off again.

"I thought she was crazy," he said heavily. "All this talk about bats and things. But I might have known better. Somebody tried to poison her this spring. I suppose you know about that?"

"She told me herself."

Carlton looked stunned.

"Are you telling me she went to the police?"

"I am. I saw her last Monday, and I sent Miss Adams at her request. She believed that someone in this house was trying to scare her into a heart attack—and death."

"That's absurd." He lit a cigarette with unsteady fingers. "Who would try a thing like that? It's silly on the face of it."

He looked profoundly shocked, however. Hilda, watching him, thought that for the first time he was really apprehensive. But the inspector shifted his questions.

"Do you know the combination of the safe?"

"No."

"Who benefits by her death?"

"That's the hell of it. We all do."

"Even the servants?"

"I'm not certain. I haven't seen her will. Her lawyer has it, Charles Willis. They may get a little. Not enough to matter."

"Have you any idea of the size of the estate?"

The shift had brought some color back to Carlton's face. He put out his cigarette and straightened.

"I don't know, and that's a fact," he said bitterly. "My father left about three million dollars. She must have quite a lot left. I wasn't in her confidence. I tried to talk to her, about her taxes and so on, but she wouldn't listen. She always thought I was a fool about money. But lately she's been cutting down expenses. I don't know why. She should have had a fair income."

"What do you mean by fair?"

"Oh, forty or fifty thousand a year."

The inspector smiled faintly. To him that amount represented capital, not income. There was a brief silence. Hilda looked at her wrist watch. It was half past four, and the early June dawn was already outlining the trees outside the windows. When the inspector spoke again his face was grave.

"The medical examiner sets the time of death as approximately between one and two o'clock. Nearer one, he thinks. He may be able to tell us more accurately after the autopsy. The only person known to have entered your mother's room during that time was yourself, Mr. Fairbanks."

Carlton leaped to his feet.

"I never touched her," he said shrilly. "I thought she was asleep. Ask Miss Adams. I wasn't in the room more than a minute or two."

He was in deadly earnest now, and cold sober. Hilda felt sorry for him. Of all the family, she thought, he was the only one outside of Jan who had had any affection for the old lady. Marian had resented her, had blamed her for the failure of her marriage. Susie had frankly flouted her. Even Eileen had called her an old devil.

"You went into the room, walked around the foot of the bed, turned off the radio, came back and closed the closet door. That right?"

"That's right."

He would not change his story, and at last he was allowed to go. The inspector looked at Hilda. "True or false?" he said.

"Partly true, anyhow. If he closed the closet door, who opened it? He's keeping something back. Something he's not going to tell."

"Any idea what it is?"

"Not the slightest. Unless he knows his wife was outside in the rain. He's very much in love with her."

He got out the knife and laid it, still in its cellophane envelope, on the table beside him.

"Let's show this to Maggie," he said.

But Maggie, having worked herself into a fine state of indignation, repudiated it at once.

"It's none of mine," she said. "And I'd like to say that I've been in this house for twenty years and never before—"

"All right," said the inspector. "Get out and send in the butler and the other woman, Ida. And make some coffee. I've got some men who need it, too."

Maggie, considerably deflated, went out, and William and Ida came in. Neither of them recognized the knife, both had been in bed when Susie's shrieks wakened them, both were—according to the inspector's comment after they left—pure as the driven snow and innocent as unborn babes.

"But behaving according to rule," he said dryly. "Always more emotional than the family in a crisis. Watch it sometime."

Susie bore this out when she was sent for. She looked faintly amused as she wandered in, a cigarette in her fingers and her raincoat still covering her draggled dressing-gown.

"I suppose the dirty work begins now," she said, sitting on the edge of the table and ignoring the knife. "I didn't like her. I've had to take her charity and her insults ever since Carl's business failed. I thought she was an old bitch and I've said it. So I suppose I'm the leading suspect."

The inspector eyed her, the nightgown, the stained bedroom slippers, her hair still damp and straight.

"Not necessarily," he said dryly. "I'd like to know why you were out in the rain tonight."

"Your lady friend has told you, hasn't she? I went out to get some cigarettes from the car, and that damned storm caught me."

"There were cigarettes all over your room, Mrs. Fairbanks. I saw them there. I don't believe that was the reason you were outside."

Susie stared at him.

"So what?" she said defiantly. "I didn't kill her, if that's what you want to know."

"But you admit you didn't like her."

"Good God! I don't like you, but I don't intend to cut your throat."

"That's very reassuring," he told her gravely. "And I haven't accused you of killing your mother-in-law. I want to know if you were in Mrs. Garrison's room tonight?"

Susie's surprise was apparently genuine.

"Eileen's? I should say not. I sat in the hall while Miss Adams fastened her screen. She was asleep, thank God. That's as near as I came to her, and nearer than I wanted to be."

"You don't like her, either?"

"She's another bitch," said Susie with feeling.

But she was evasive after that. Hilda, watching her, was certain she was frightened, that her assurance covered something close to panic. She stuck to her story, however. She had gone out for cigarettes and the storm had caught her. The garage was locked, as was the door to the stairs leading to Amos's quarters. She had stood under the eaves of the building for a while. Then she had made a dash for the house.

"That's all?"

"That's all," she said defiantly.

The inspector took a piece of paper from his pocket and unfolded it.

"'At five minutes before two,'" he read, "'a woman yelped under my window. I raised it and looked out. She was standing still, but someone else was going out through the break in the fence. I think it was a man. The woman was Mrs. Carlton Fairbanks. She was rubbing her arm. I watched her until she went back to the house.'"

Susie's bravado was gone. She pushed back her heavy hair.

"Amos, the dirty skunk!" she said. "All right, I wasn't going to say anything, but I can't help you at that. There was a man there. I was trying the door to the stairs when he grabbed me by the arm. I yelled and he beat it. But I don't know who it was."

She stuck to that. He had been behind her when he caught her. He hadn't spoken, and the rain was like a cloudburst. All she knew was that he let go of her when she screamed, and disappeared. She hadn't said anything to Miss Adams. No use scaring a woman who had to be up all night. She had meant to tell Carl, but he was asleep and snoring. But she had had a shock. She hadn't felt like going to bed. She had sat in the hall, and then Mrs. Fairbanks had been killed.

She pulled back the sleeve of her raincoat and showed her forearm.

"Take a look at that if you don't believe me," she said.

There were two or three small bruises on her arm, as if made by fingers, and they were already turning purple.

"I bruise easy," she said.

Nothing shook her story. The sun had risen and birds were chirping outside when at last she was dismissed. With a warning, however.

"I think you know who the man was, Mrs. Fairbanks," the inspector said soberly. "I want you to think it over. It is bad business to keep anything back in a case of this sort."

She went out, and he looked at Hilda.

"All right, Miss Pinkerton," he said. "What about it?"

"She's a fine actress and a pretty fair liar," Hilda said. "She's protecting somebody." She hesitated. "It may be the doctor. He lives across Huston Street, and he uses that break in the fence. But it might have been innocent enough. He's in love with Jan Garrison. He may have meant to meet her. Or even"—she smiled faintly—"to look up at her window. I believe people in love do things like that."

The inspector, however, had jumped to his feet.

"The doctor!" he said. "He's in love with the girl, she inherits under the will, and he was alone outside Mrs. Fairbanks's door for fifteen or twenty minutes. Where the hell is he?"

"He took an injured woman to the hospital. He may be home now. But he couldn't have done it. The radio—"

"Oh, blast the radio," he said.

He went out into the hall and sent an officer to Courtney Brooke's house. After that he sent for Janice. She came in slowly, her eyes still red, and Hilda felt a wave of pity for her. Before going to bed she had wrapped the long ends of her hair in curlers, and they made her look childish and naïve. Even the inspector spoke gently.

"Sit down, Miss Garrison," he said. "You know we have to ask all sorts of questions in a case like this. You needn't be afraid. All we want is the truth."

"I don't know anything."

"I don't suppose you do. You were asleep when it happened, weren't you?"

"I don't know when it happened, but I wasn't asleep when Susie yelled. I wasn't sleepy, and Granny's radio had been turned on full."

"You hadn't expected to go out? Into the grounds, I mean."

Jan looked puzzled.

"Out? No. Why should I?"

"Let's say, to meet someone?"

It took her by surprise. She stared at him. Then a look of horror spread over her face. She looked wildly about the room, at Hilda, at the door. She even half rose from her chair.

"I don't know what you mean," she managed to gasp.

The inspector's voice was still quiet.

"Suppose you meant to meet someone by the garage. Then it rained, and you didn't go. That would be understandable, wouldn't it? He came, but you didn't."

"Nobody came. I don't know what you're talking about."

"Would you swear on oath that you had no appointment to meet Doctor Brooke by the garage tonight?"

She only looked bewildered.

"Doctor Brooke!" she said. "Certainly not. He can see me whenever he wants to, here in the house."

He let her go, watching her out with a puzzled look on his face.

"Well, what scared her?" he demanded. "Do I look as formidable as all that, or— What about this Amos, anyhow? Think he's reliable?"

"He's a mischiefmaker. Stubborn and sly. He's probably honest enough."

"What is 'honest enough'?" he inquired quizzically.

But Hilda was thinking. She was remembering Jan's story that Courtney Brooke had seen her father outside the fence a night or two before. That, she was convinced, had been behind Jan's terror just now. Yet there were so many other things that she felt dizzy. The coldness for a day or so between Carlton and Susie, and Susie's fainting. Her idiotic story about going to the garage for cigarettes. Carlton, earlier in the week, carrying something from the stable and being locked out. The bats and so on in Mrs. Fairbanks's room, and the closet door which opened and closed itself.

They must make a pattern of some sort. Only what had they to do with an old woman dead of a knife thrust in a closed and guarded room?

It was just before young Brooke's arrival that one of the detectives from upstairs came down and stood in the doorway. He looked rather sheepish.

"There's a bat in that room where the old lady was," he said. "It was hanging to a curtain, and it acts like it's going crazy."

"It hasn't a thing on me," said the inspector, and sighed.

It was bright daylight when Courtney Brooke arrived. He looked tired and puzzled, and like Susie he showed evidence of having been caught in the storm. His collar was crumpled and his necktie a limp string.

"What's wrong?" he said. "I've just come back from the hospital. Is Mrs. Fairbanks—"

"Mrs. Fairbanks is dead," said the inspector dryly. "She was murdered last night."

The doctor stiffened and looked wildly at Hilda.

"Murdered! All I ordered for her was a sleeping tablet if she couldn't sleep. If she got anything else—"

"She was stabbed. Not poisoned."

The full impact seemed to strike him with that. He sat down, as though his legs would not hold him.

"I'd like an account of what you were doing last night, doctor," said the inspector smoothly. "Begin, if you please, with Mrs. Garrison's trouble, when you were sent for. You decided to give her a hypodermic. Then what?"

He made an effort to collect himself.

"I didn't notice the time. She was having pain. She was afraid of a miscarriage. I asked the nurse here to get me some sterile water. She went downstairs. It took some time, and I—"

"You remained outside Mrs. Fairbanks's door during all that time?"

He looked unhappy.

"Well, yes and no," he said. "I went back and spoke to Janice Garrison. She had been uneasy about her father. Her stepmother said he had left her, but she didn't believe it. She thought something had happened to him."

"Did you stay in the hall? Or did you go into Miss Garrison's room?"

"I went in. I was there only a minute or two. Long enough to reassure her."

Hilda spoke.

"You agreed to guard the door," she said. "Like Cerberus. You remember?"

"Well, look," he said reasonably. "Only the family was in the house. Nobody would have had time to get in from the outside. And it was poison she was afraid of. Not—being stabbed." He became suddenly conscious of his appearance. He put a hand to his collar. "Sorry I look like this," he said. "The fellow who brought me was on the steps. He wouldn't let me in the house."

The inspector eyed him.

"Never mind how you look. This isn't a party. It's a murder investigation." He cleared his throat. "That's all, is it? You stepped into Miss Garrison's room and out again. Right?"

"I might have been there five minutes," he admitted. "I'd been telephoning around for her, and—"

"You saw nothing whatever that might be useful? Nobody moving about?"

For an instant he seemed to hesitate, and Hilda remembered the coffee spilled in the saucer and his strange expression as she came up the stairs. But he shook his head.

"Nothing," he said.

He had gone home after giving Eileen the hypodermic, he said. It was raining a little, and he had taken the short cut by the stable and the break in the fence. He saw no one lurking there. And he was in bed asleep when a man from Joe's Market rang the bell and said a woman had had an accident at the corner.

"What time was that?"

About two, he thought. It was storming hard by that time. He had telephoned for an ambulance, taken his bag, and gone to the corner. The woman was lying on the pavement, with one or two people with her. She was pretty badly hurt. He had done what he could, and then gone with the ambulance to the hospital.

"I stayed while they operated," he said. "It's my old hospital, Mount Hope. They all knew me."

"At ten minutes to two you were in bed?"

"I was in bed when this fellow rang the bell. I opened a window and he called up to me."

"You were undressed?"

Brooke grinned.

"I'll say I was. I haven't got much on now, under this suit."

"You didn't run into Mrs. Susie Fairbanks, at the garage at five minutes to two, and catch hold of her?"

He looked astounded.

"Good God, no! Why should I?"

But he lost some of his spontaneity after that. He was wary. He answered the routine questions more carefully, and at last the inspector shrugged and let him go. He was irritable, however.

"What's the idea?" he said to Hilda grumpily. "That fellow knows something. Everybody around here knows something—except me. Even you, probably." He looked at her keenly. "I

wouldn't put it past you, you know. You've held out on me before."

"Only when I thought it was necessary," she said, smiling up
at him delicately.

But he had enough. He had had too much. He got up and
banged the table.

"God damn it, Hilda," he roared. "If I thought you have any
pets around here and are protecting them, I'd—I'd turn you over
my knee."

14.

It was eight o'clock in the morning before they could rouse Eileen enough to be interviewed. Carlton, unshaven and still only partially dressed, was at the telephone trying to locate his sister. Susie had brought him a cup of coffee, but it sat untouched beside him.

"Hello. That you, Blanche? Sorry to bother you. Did Marian happen to tell you where she was going to stop while she's away? It's rather urgent."

He would hang up after a minute or two, feverishly thumb the telephone book and commence all over again.

In the morning room Courtney Brooke was trying to comfort Jan, a Jan who lay face down on a long davenport and refused to be comforted. One of the curlers on the end of her long bob had come loose, and he sat turning the soft curl over a finger.

"Believe me, darling, it's all right. You mustn't go on like this. You break my heart, sweet."

"Granny's dead." Her voice was smothered. "Nothing can change that."

"It's a bad business, Jan. I know that. Only try to face it as it is, not as you're afraid it is. You're not being fair. Even the police don't condemn people until they have the facts."

"I saw him. I spoke to him." She turned over and sat up, her eyes wide with fear. "Now it will all come out, Court. She had it in the safe. She told me so. They'll open it, and—then they'll know."

"Whoever did it didn't open the safe. It's still there, sweet."

She got up, and as he steadied her he thought how thin she was, how badly life had treated her. His arm tightened around her.

"If it's still there," she said excitedly. "Do you think we could get it? Oh, Court, can't we get it? She must have had the combination somewhere. She never trusted her memory."

"We can make a try anyhow. Able to get upstairs?"

"I could fly, if I thought it would help."

They were a sorry-looking pair as they went up the long staircase, Jan's eyes still swollen, her rumpled nightgown under her bathrobe, her feet still bare. Young Brooke was not much better, a disreputable figure in a suit which had been soaked with rain, his hair standing wildly in all directions, and his collar melted around his neck. They did not notice the uniformed man in the lower hall, standing stolidly on guard, and there was hope in both of them until they reached the upper hall, to confront a policeman parked outside Mrs. Fairbanks's door, smoking a surreptitious cigarette.

He put it out quickly, so he did not see the dismay in their faces.

Brooke left soon after that. Eileen was still sleeping. The house was quiet. But outside in the grounds one or two men were quietly examining the pillars and roof of the porte-cochere, and a detective in plain clothes and bent double was going carefully over the ground around the stable and near the fence.

He looked up as the doctor neared him.

"Got permission to leave the place?"

"I'm the doctor," Brooke said stiffly. "My office is across the street. Anything to say about that?"

He was in a fighting mood, but the detective only grinned.

"Not a word, brother. Not a word. Might like a look at your feet. That's all."

"What the hell are my feet to you?"

"Not a thing. You could lose 'em both and I wouldn't shed a tear. Lemme look at those shoes, doc."

Brooke was seething, but after a glance at the shoes, especially the soles, the detective only shrugged.

"Went out of here after the rain started, didn't you?" he said. "All right. That checks. I'll see you later. Those shoes could stand some work on them."

Brooke was still furious as he started across the street. For the first time he realized the excitement in the neighborhood. There was a large crowd around the entrance to the driveway on Grove Avenue, and the windows on both streets were filled with men in their shirt sleeves, and women hastily or only partially dressed. To add to his rage the slovenly girl from the house where he had his offices was on the steps, surrounded by a group of laughing boys.

He caught one of them and shook him.

"Get out of here," he said. "Get out and stay out, all of you." He jerked the girl to her feet. "Go inside and do some work, for once," he ordered. "If I catch you out here again—"

He knew it was useless. It was the ugly side of all tragedy, this morbid curiosity and avid interest which deprived even grief of privacy. But he could not fight it. He went upstairs and took a bath, as though to wash it away.

In the dining-room at the Fairbanks house the inspector was eating a substantial Sunday morning breakfast of sausages and pancakes, and a long rangy captain of the homicide squad was trying to keep up with him. Hilda, unable to eat, eyed them resentfully. Men were like that, she thought. They did not project themselves into other people's troubles as women did. All this was just a case, a case and a job. It did not matter that a family was being torn apart, or that some one member of it was probably headed for the chair.

William had brought in a fresh supply of pancakes when Amos came in. His small, sly eyes were gleaming.

"Fellow out in the yard says to tell you he's got a footprint," he said. "It's under the big oak, and he's got a soapbox over it."

The captain got up, eyeing his last pancake ruefully.

"I guess you win, inspector," he said. "Thirteen to my eleven. I suppose you'll want a cast."

He went out, and the inspector took a final sip of coffee and put down his napkin.

"I'm feeling stronger," he announced. "Nothing like food to take the place of sleep."

"I should think you could stay awake for the next month," said Hilda tartly.

He got up and lit a cigarette.

"Don't be crabbed," he said. "It doesn't suit you. You are the ministering angel, the lady who knits while people pour out their troubles to her. Which reminds me, how about the Garrison woman? I'll have to see her. What do you think of her?"

"As a suspect? All I can say is that women don't usually murder when they're threatened with a miscarriage and under the influence of morphia."

"Don't they?" He eyed her with interest. "How much you know! But you'd be surprised, my Hilda. You'd be surprised at what some women can do."

Eileen was still in her drugged sleep when Hilda, leaving him outside, went into her room. It was not easy to rouse her, and when she did waken she seemed not to know where she was. She sat up in bed, looking dazedly around her.

"How on earth did I get here?" she demanded, blinking in the light.

"You came last night. Don't you remember?"

She stretched and yawned. Then she smiled maliciously.

"My God, do I remember!" she said. "Did you see their faces?"

But she was not smiling when the inspector came in. She sat up and drawing the bedclothing around her stared at him suspiciously.

"Who are you?" she said. "I don't know you, do I?"

He looked down at her. A neurotic, he thought, and scared to death. Heaven keep him from neurotic women.

"I'm sorry, Mrs. Garrison. I am a police officer. I want to ask you a few questions."

But he did not ask her any questions just then. She seemed profoundly shocked as full recollection came back to her. She looked indeed as though she might faint again, and when at last she lay back, shivering under the bedclothes, she could tell him nothing at all.

"I remember Susie screaming. I got up and went to the door. Somebody said Mrs. Fairbanks was dead—murdered. I guess I fainted after that."

"Did you hear anyone in this room last night? Before it happened."

"I don't know when it happened," she said petulantly. "Ida was here, and the doctor. And the nurse, of course."

"Did you unhook the window screen over there, for any purpose?"

She went pale.

"My screen?" she said. "Do you mean—"

"It was open. Miss Adams heard it banging. She came in and closed it."

Suddenly she sat up in bed, wide-eyed and terrified.

"I want to get out of here," she said. "I'm sick, and I don't know anything about it. I wouldn't have come if I'd had any other place to go. They'd pin this murder on me if they could. They all hate me."

"Who hates you?"

"All of them," she said wildly, and burst into loud hysterical crying.

It was some time before he could question her further. But she protested that she had not even heard the radio, and that Mrs. Fairbanks had been as usual when she talked to her.

"She didn't seem nervous or apprehensive?"

"She seemed unpleasant. She never liked me. But she did promise to look after me when my—when my baby came."

She made no objection when he asked to take her fingerprints. "Part of the routine," he told her. She lay passive on her pillows while he rolled one finger after another on the card. But she did object when he asked her to stay in the house for a day or two longer.

"I'm better," she said. "I'm all right. The doctor said—"

"I'll let you go as soon as possible," he told her, and went out.

It was in the hall outside her door that Hilda remembered

about the figure at the top of the third floor stairs. The inspector was about to light a cigarette. He blew out the match and stared at her.

"Why in God's name didn't you tell me that before?" he demanded furiously.

She flushed. "You might remember that I've had a murder on my hands, and a lot of hysterical people. I just forgot it."

He was still indignant, however. He went up the stairs, with Hilda following. But nothing was changed. The guest rooms with their drawn shades were as she had last seen them; the hall stretched back to the servants' quarters, empty and undisturbed. A brief examination showed all the windows closed and locked, and the inspector, wiping his dusty hands, looked skeptical.

"Sure you didn't dream it?"

"I came up and looked around. There wasn't time for anyone to have gone back to the servants' rooms. I thought it was Maggie or Ida, curious about Mrs. Garrison."

"When was all this?"

"Before I went down to boil the water for the hypodermic. I was gone only a minute or two. I hardly left the top of the stairs."

He was still ruffled as he went back along the hall. There were closets there, a cedar room, and a trunk room. All of them were neat and dustless, and none showed any signs of recent use as a hiding place. He lit matches, examined floors, and, still ignoring Hilda, went on back to the servants' quarters. Compared with the rest of the house they were musty, with the closeness of such places even in June, the closed windows, the faint odor of cooking from below, of long-worn clothing, and unmade beds.

Two of the rooms were empty, but Ida was in hers. She was

sitting by a window, her hands folded in her lap and a queer look on her long thin face as Hilda went in.

"I was nervous and Maggie sent me up," she said. "But there's no use of my going to bed. I couldn't sleep."

It was the appearance of the inspector which definitely terrified her, however. She went white to the lips. She tried to get up and then sank back in her chair.

"What is it?" she asked. "I don't know anything. What do you want with me? Can't I get a little rest?"

Hilda tried to quiet her.

"It hasn't anything to do with Mrs. Fairbanks's death, Ida," she said. "I thought I saw someone in the upper hall last night, before—before it happened. If it was you it's all right. We're only checking up."

Ida shook her head.

"It wasn't me, miss."

"Would it have been William? Or Maggie?"

She was quieter now.

"I wouldn't know about that. They usually sleep like the dead."

But Hilda was remembering something. She was seeing the household gather after Susie screamed, and seeing Maggie and William come along the back hall on the second floor, while Ida was standing still, looking down from the front stairs to the third floor. She did not mention it. Quite possibly, Ida as the housemaid used those stairs habitually. She tucked it away in her memory, however, to wonder later if she should have told it. If it would have changed anything, or altered the inevitable course of events.

Neither of them could change Ida's story. She sat there, twisting her work-worn hands in her lap. She had been in bed. She had seen nobody, and she had liked the old lady. She had looked after her as well as she could. Tears welled in her eyes, and the inspector left her there and went out, muttering to himself.

"Damn all crying women," he said. "I'm fed up with them."

That was when he timed Hilda, making her leave her chair in the hall, go up, look around for a light switch, and come down again. He put his watch back in his pocket and looked at her. grimly.

"Three minutes," he said. "A lot can happen in three minutes, my girl."

He left at nine o'clock, driving away with his uniformed chauffeur. The men who had been scattered over the grounds had disappeared, but one officer was on duty on Huston Street beside the break in the fence. Another was holding back the crowd at the gate, and two still remained in the house. Hilda watched the difficulty with which the car made its way through the crowd.

"It's disgusting," she said to the tall young policeman on duty in the lower hall. "They ought to be ashamed."

He smiled indulgently.

"They like a bit of excitement, miss." He smiled. "There's a lot of reporters out there, too. I caught one carrying in the milk bottles early this morning."

As she went up the stairs she could still hear Carlton at the library phone.

"Hello, George. I'm trying to locate Marian. She's out of town somewhere. I suppose you and Nell haven't heard from her?"

15.

She was very tired. When she looked into Eileen's room Ida was running a carpet sweeper over the floor. Eileen's hair had been combed and fresh linen put on her bed. She looked better, although she was still pale.

"If you're all right I'll go to bed for an hour or two, Mrs. Garrison," Hilda said. "I haven't had much sleep lately."

"I'm perfectly all right. I told that fool of a policeman, but he wouldn't listen."

Hilda went back toward her room. But she did not go to bed. Maggie was carrying a tray into Jan's room, and she followed her. Jan was standing by a window, fully dressed. She looked at the tray and shook her head.

"I'm afraid I can't eat," she said. "Thanks, anyhow. I'll have the coffee."

Maggie put down the tray firmly.

"You'll eat," she said. "Somebody's got to keep going around here." Her voice softened. "Try it anyhow, dearie," she said. "Just remember she was old. She hadn't long anyhow."

Jan's chin quivered.

"She liked living."

"Well, so do we all," said Maggie, philosophically. "That don't mean we can go on forever."

She went out. Jan looked at Hilda.

"I've been trying to think. How are we to get word to Mother? I don't suppose it is in the papers, is it?"

"I hardly think so. There wasn't time."

"And there are no evening papers today," Jan said desperately. "She may not hear it until tomorrow. And she ought to be here. Uncle Carl's no good at that sort of thing, and Susie's asleep. I went in and she was dead to the world. I wanted to talk to her. I—"

Her voice trailed off. Her hands shook as she tried to pour the coffee. Hilda took the miniature pot from her and poured it for her.

"Why not waken her?" she said quietly. "After all, if it's important—"

"Important!" Jan's voice was bitter. "You've seen her. You've heard her. You know she hated Granny. She hated living in the house with her. Uncle Carl wanted a farm, and she adores him. They can have it now," she added hopelessly. "They'll have her money. First she tried to scare Granny to death, and when that wasn't any good—"

"What do you mean by that?" Hilda demanded sharply. "Scaring her to death."

"Those bats and things. You don't think they got in by themselves!" Jan was scornful. "It was just the sort of thing she would think of. Scare Granny out of the house, or into a heart attack. What did she care?"

Hilda was thoughtful. In a way Jan was right. Susie was quite capable of it. It might even appeal to her macabre sense of humor. The murder, however, was different. She could not see Susie putting arsenic in the old lady's sugar or driving a knife into her heart.

"She had the chance last night, too," Jan went on. "She could have heard Courtney come back to talk to me while you were downstairs. She could have slipped through Uncle Carl's room and around the screen. Nobody would have seen her."

She stopped, looking startled. Susie was in the doorway, cigarette in hand and her sharp blue eyes blazing.

"So I did it!" she said. "You little idiot, didn't I lie my head off last night for you?" She threw back the sleeve of her dressing-gown and showed her arm. "You know who did that, don't you? Suppose I'd told the police your precious father was here in the grounds last night? And his wife inside the house with the screen over the porte-cochere open? Suppose I'd said that the whole thing was a plant to get Eileen into this house, so Frank Garrison could get in, too?"

Hilda watched them, her blue eyes shrewd. Neither of them seemed aware of her presence. She saw that Jan was on the verge of collapse.

"He wouldn't kill Granny. Never. You know it. Deep down in your heart you know it."

Susie eyed her. Then she shrugged.

"All right, kid," she said. "I didn't tell the police. I won't, either, unless you go around yelling that I did it. Or Carlton." Suddenly she sent a shocked look at Hilda. "Good, God, I forgot. You're police yourself, aren't you?"

"Not all the time. I'm a human being, too." Hilda smiled faintly.

"Well, forget it," said Susie. "I was just talking. The kid here made me mad. Maybe he thought Eileen was here. He might have come to find out."

She went back to her room, and Jan caught Hilda by the arm.

"That's why he came," she said desperately. "I swear it is. I'll swear it by anything holy. My window was up, and he called to me. He said, 'Jan, do you know where Eileen has gone? She's not in the apartment.' When I told him she was here and—and sick, he seemed worried. But he wouldn't come in. He went away again, in the rain. In the rain," she repeated, as though the fact hurt her. "I can't even telephone him," she went on. "Uncle Carl's still using it. And if the police find it out—"

"Why worry about that? He had no reason for wishing your grandmother—out of the way, had he?"

"Of course not." She lit a cigarette and smoked it feverishly. "He was devoted to her. But he doesn't know what's happened. He ought to know. He ought to be able to protect himself. Look," she said, putting down the cigarette, "would you be willing to tell him? To go there and tell him? It wouldn't do any harm. He can't run away. That's all I want, for him to know."

It was a long time before Hilda agreed, but the girl's sick face and passionate anxiety finally decided her. Also she was curious. There was something behind all this, something more than a distracted husband trying in the middle of the night to locate a missing wife. Why had he not come in when he learned that Eileen was sick? Surely that would have been the normal thing to do.

She knew she had very little time. The police had the cast of the footprint under the oak. They would be working on it now. They would have examined the shoes of the men in the house, measured them, perhaps photographed them. And if Amos knew more than he had told—

She hurried to her room to dress. As she opened the door she had the feeling that something had moved rapidly across the floor. Whatever it was she could not find it, and she dressed rapidly and went down the stairs. Evidently the officer there had no orders to hold her, for he smiled and opened the door.

"Out for a walk?"

"I need some air," she said blandly.

Under the porte-cochere, however, she stopped. The crowd was still on the pavement, held back by the guard, and a photographer was holding up his camera. She turned quickly toward the stable and the broken fence. Amos was not in sight, but the soapbox lay on its side under the oak tree, some fifty feet away. She hurried to the break in the fence, and straightened, to look into the lens of a camera. A grinning young man thanked her. She made a wild snatch at the camera, but he evaded it.

"Naughty, naughty," he said. "Papa slap. Now, what's your name, please?"

"I have no name," she told him furiously.

"Must be a disadvantage at times. How do they get you? Say, 'Here, you'?"

He took another flash of her indignant face before she could stop him, and she was moving rapidly toward the corner when she became aware that the crowd was coming toward her. It moved slowly but irresistibly, as though propelled by some unseen power from behind. A half-dozen small boys ran ahead of it.

"That's the nurse!" one of them yelled. "She's got her cap off, but I know her."

"Hey, nurse! What's happened in there?"

The reporters were in the lead now. In an instant she was surrounded by eager young faces. She could see her bus a block away, and she stood haughtily silent, like a small neat Pekinese among a throng of disorderly street dogs. "Have a heart, sister." "Come on, how was the old lady killed?" "Has anyone been arrested?"

She was driven to speech, in sheer desperation.

"I have nothing to say," she told them. "If you care to follow me while I get some fresh uniforms and look after my canary, that's all the good it will do you."

They laughed but persisted until the bus came and she got on. Looking back she could see them, returning discouraged to take up their stations again, to wait and hope for a break, to be able perhaps to get a new angle on the story and maybe a raise in salary. She felt unhappy and guilty, as though she had failed them. As, of course, she had.

She reached the Garrison apartment at ten o'clock. No one answered the bell, and at last she tried the door. It was unlocked, and she stepped inside, to find herself in a long gallery, paved with black-and-white marble, and with a fine old tapestry hung at the end. It surprised her, as did the drawing-room when she saw it; a handsome room carefully furnished, but with every sign of extreme neglect. The grand piano showed dust in the morning sun, the brocaded curtains were awry, the windows filthy, the rugs askew on the floor. Old magazines and papers lay about, and a vase of flowers on a table had been dead and dried for days.

Her tidy soul revolted. No wonder men left women who surrounded themselves with dirt and disorder. But there was no sign of Frank Garrison. The place was quiet and apparently empty. Not until she had investigated most of the apartment did she locate him, in a small room at the far end of the gallery. He was in a deep chair, and he was sound asleep.

Whatever she had expected it was not this. She inspected him carefully. He was in pajamas and bathrobe, and the Sunday papers were scattered around him. A cluttered ash tray and an empty coffee cup were beside him, and he had the exhausted, unshaven look of a man who had slept little or not at all the night before.

When she touched him on the shoulder he jerked awake. Not fully, however.

"Sorry," he mumbled. "Guess I dozed off." He looked up at her and blinked.

"Thought you were my wife," he said. "My apologies." He got up slowly, his big body still clumsy with sleep. Then he recognized her. He looked alarmed.

"Miss Adams! Has anything happened? Is Jan—"

"Jan's all right." She sat down. "I have other news for you, Mr. Garrison, unless you already know it. Jan wanted me to tell you. Mrs. Fairbanks is dead."

He looked surprised.

"Dead!" he said. "Just like that! Jan will take it hard. Still, I suppose it was to be expected." He looked down at his pajamas. "I'd better dress and go over. I didn't expect a visitor. What was it? Heart, I suppose."

"No," said Hilda.

"No? Then what—"

"She was murdered, Mr. Garrison."

He stared at her. He had been in the act of picking up a cigarette. Now his hand hung frozen over the box. The incredulity in his face gave way to sick horror.

"Murdered!" he said hoarsely. "I don't understand. Not poison again?"

"She was stabbed. With a knife."

He seemed still unable to take it in.

"I don't understand," he repeated. "Who would kill her? She hadn't very long to live. And nobody hated her. Even the servants—"

He did not finish. He got up and went to the window.

"Is Jan all right?" he asked without turning.

"She's worried, Mr. Garrison."

He swung around.

"Worried! What do you mean, worried?"

"You were outside the house last night, and Mrs. Carlton Fairbanks knows it."

"Susie! So it was Susie!" he said, and gave a short laugh. "She scared the insides out of me."

"Jan thought you ought to know," Hilda said patiently. "There may be trouble. The police have found a footprint. I imagine it's yours. I promised to tell you before they got here—if they come at all. Susie won't talk, but Amos might. He looked out the window. He may have recognized you."

He began to see the seriousness of his situation. Yet his story was coherent and straightforward. He had had what he called a difference with Eileen, on Wednesday night. He had packed a bag and gone to his club, and on Saturday morning he had taken a plane to Washington.

"Things haven't been very good," he said. "I needed a job, and I thought with all this government housing I might get something. I happen to be an architect. But it was a Saturday, and summer"—he smiled—"the government doesn't work on June week-ends."

He had got back to the apartment late the night before to find Eileen gone and her suitcase missing. They had had to let the maid go, and he didn't know what had happened to Eileen.

"I thought Jan might know," he said. "But I didn't want to telephone her and rouse the house. So I went over. It was one o'clock when I left there. I've done that before, talked to Jan at night, I mean. Her window was up, although it was raining cats and dogs, and I called to her. She said my wife was there, so I came back here."

"Meeting Susie on the way?"

"Meeting Susie on the way," he said, and smiled again. "She yelled like an Indian."

She considered that. It might be true. She had an idea, however, that it was not all the truth.

"You didn't go back again? To the house?" He looked at her oddly.

"See here," he said. "What's all this about? They don't think *I* killed the old lady, do they?"

"Somebody killed her," Hilda said dryly, and got up.

He saw her out, apologizing for the dust, the evident disorder. He owned the place. He couldn't sell it, worse luck. Nobody could sell anything nowadays, even a tapestry. But she felt that behind all this, his confident manner, the composure on his good-looking face, his mind was far away, working hard and fast.

She was on a corner waiting for a bus when she saw the inspector's car drive up to the door of the apartment building and two or three men get out. So Amos had talked, after all.

She was not surprised, on her return to the Fairbanks house, to learn from William that the police had taken away the window screen from Eileen's room. But she was rather astonished to find Carlton, in a morning coat and striped trousers, and wearing a black tie, wandering around upstairs and carrying a hammer and an old cigar box filled with nails.

"Thought I'd nail up the other screens," he said vaguely. "Can't have people getting in and out of the house. Not safe."

He went into Eileen's room, a dapper, incongruous figure, and Hilda followed him. Eileen was sitting up in bed. She looked better, although she was still pale; and she managed an ironical smile when Carlton told her what he was doing.

"You're a little late with that, aren't you?" she said.

"Some of us still want to live, Eileen."

"You can do that now, can't you?" she said maliciously. "Live the way you like, get your Susie safe on a farm away from other men, raise pigs, do anything you damn well please."

He stiffened.

"That was entirely uncalled for. If you were not a sick woman—"

"If I were not a sick woman I wouldn't be here."

He finished his hammering, and later Hilda, remembering that day, was to hear the noise as he moved from room to room, and even to smell the putty and white paint with which he neatly covered the signs of his labors.

He finished at eleven-thirty, which was almost exactly the time Fuller and his henchmen were leaving Frank Garrison. He had told a straight story, but the inspector was not satisfied. He stood in the long marble-floored gallery and put his hat on with a jerk.

"I'll ask you not to leave town," he said. "Outside of that, of course, you're free. I suppose you have no idea where your first wife is? We'd like to locate her."

"I am not in her confidence," he said stiffly. "I would be the last person to know."

16.

From: *Commanding Officer, 17th Precinct*
To: *Medical Examiner*
Subject: *Death of Eliza Douglas Fairbanks, of Ten Grove Avenue.*
   1. On June 15, 1941, at 2:15 a.m. a report was received from Inspector Harlan Fuller that a Mrs. Eliza Douglas Fairbanks, aged 72 years, had been found dead in her bed as a result of a stab wound in the chest.
   2. Case was reported at once by Inspector Fuller and usual steps taken. Inspector Fuller and Captain Henderson of homicide squad were assigned to case.

The inspector had this document in front of him that noon. In such brief fashion, he thought, were the tragedies of life reported. Men and women died of violence. Tragedy wrecked homes. Hatred and greed and revenge took their toll. And each of them could be officially recorded in less than a hundred words.

Nor was the report of the autopsy more human. An old woman had died, cruelly and unnecessarily. Died in a closed room, with access to it almost impossible. And the autopsy, after recording her pathetic age, her shrunken weight, and the entirely useless examination of her head, abdomen, and thorax, merely reported the cause of death as an incised wound with a tract of two and one-half inches, which on being carefully dissected was shown to have reached the heart. And that the approximate time of death had been between twelve-thirty and one-thirty in the morning.

He put it down. After all, murder was an inhuman business, he thought, and began again to look over the reports and his own memoranda which had accumulated on the desk. Considering that the day was Sunday they covered considerable ground.

The house: *No sign of entrance by roof of porte-cochere. Blurred prints on window screen, one identified as belonging to Miss Adams, nurse. Three ladders on property, none showing signs of having been out in the rain. No indication pillars had been climbed. All doors and windows on lower floor closed and locked. No phonograph or remote control for radio found. Knife not belonging to kitchen. (Evidence of one Margaret O'Neil, cook.) At seat of crime fingerprints only of dead woman, servants and family, including those of Mrs. Eileen Garrison on back of chair. None of Mrs. Carlton Fairbanks. Prints of Carlton Fairbanks on foot of bed and closet door. Prints of dead woman on safe. No others.*

On the people in the house at the time of the crime his notes were brief, mostly written in his own hand.

Carlton Fairbanks: *Son of deceased. Member of prosperous brokerage house until 1930. Business gradually declined until 1938, when it was liquidated. Married in 1930 to Susan Mary Kelly.*

Came to live with mother in 1938. Wife disliked by Mrs. Fairbanks and daughter Marian. Both Carlton Fairbanks and wife anxious to leave and buy farm. Is supposed to inherit, along with sister and niece, Janice Garrison, under will. Admits entering room at or about 1:15 to turn off radio.

Susan Mary Fairbanks: *See above. Reason for visit to stable-garage that night not known. Did not enter, as encountered Garrison and was scared away. No cigarettes in her car, although given as reason for night excursion. Does not conceal dislike of mother-in-law. Father contractor in small way. Family lives at 140 South Street in plain but respectable neighborhood. On good terms with them. Probably does not inherit under will but would share husband's portion.*

Marion Garrison: *Quarreled with mother and left home last Wednesday evening, June eleventh. Present address unknown. Thirty-eight years of age, thin, dark, usually dressed in black. Taxicab which called for her took her to Pennsylvania Station. No further information. According to servants, bitterly resentful over husband's second marriage. Has lived at Grove Avenue house since marriage in 1921, as mother refused to be left alone. Divorced in 1934 at Reno, Nevada.*

Janice Garrison: *Age 19. Probably inherits under will. Friendly with father and second wife. Apparently devoted to grandmother. No motive, unless money. Is supposed to be interested in Dr. Courtney Brooke.*

Courtney Allen Brooke, M.D.: *Age 28. Office and house at 13 Huston Street. Graduate Harvard Medical School. Interned two years Mount Hope Hospital. In private work one year. Small practice, barely earning expenses. First called to attend deceased March tenth, when treatment was given for arsenic poisoning. Has attended deceased at intervals since. Apparently in house during time of crime, in attendance on Mrs. Eileen Garrison, who was threatened with abortion. Alibi given by nurse Hilda Adams: the dead woman turned on her radio before his departure.*

Eileen Garrison: *Age 35. Married in 1934 to Francis J. Garrison, following divorce. Formerly governess to Janice Garrison. Small, blond, nervous temperament. Born on farm near Templeton, thirty miles from city, where parents still live. Not liked by Fairbanks family, although Janice Garrison remained friendly. Could expect nothing under will. In house at time of crime, but sick and under influence of morphine administered at or about one o'clock.*

Francis Jarvis Garrison: *Well-known architect. Age 42. Inherited money. Supposed to be wealthy until 1929. Since then heavy losses. Pays ex-wife ten thousand a year alimony, tax free. Owns large apartment, but behind on maintenance charges. Divorced in 1934. Married daughter's governess soon after. Produces ticket stub to prove plane trip to Washington Saturday. Admits being in grounds night of crime and says he talked to daughter, to learn his wife's whereabouts. Uncertain of time. Thinks between 1:30 and 2:00 a.m. Encounter with Mrs. Fairbanks, Jr. purely accidental. Admits footprint his. Expects nothing under will.*

There were brief reports on the servants, but he glanced at them casually. Only Ida's he picked up and examined.

Ida Miller: *Country girl born in Lafayette County. Age 40. Ten years in Fairbanks house. Hysterical since murder. Possibly not telling all she knows.*

He was still looking at it when the commissioner came in. The commissioner had expected to play golf, and he was in a bad humor. The inspector offered him a chair, which he took, and a cigar, which he refused.

"Never smoke them," he said. "What's all this, anyhow? I thought you'd put that woman of yours to watch the Fairbanks house."

"Not the house," said the inspector politely. "Mrs. Fairbanks herself."

"So she lets her be killed! It's the hell of a note, Fuller. I may be new to this job, but when you guarantee to protect a woman—and a prominent woman at that—I want to know why the devil she wasn't protected."

"She was, as a matter of fact. It couldn't have happened. Only it did."

"Don't give me double talk," said the commissioner, the veins in his forehead swelling. "She's dead, isn't she?"

It was some time before the inspector could tell the story. He went back to the attempt to poison Mrs. Fairbanks, and to the mystery of the bats and so on in the room.

"They got in somehow," he said. "I've been over the place. I don't see how it was done. But it was."

"Carried in," said the commissioner. "That's easy. Carried in while she was out and left there. Room wasn't locked, was it?"

"Not during the day."

"All right. Get on with it."

He sat with his eyes closed while the inspector got on with it, reading now and then from his notes. At the end he sat up, eyeing the inspector with unexpected shrewdness.

"You've got only two suspects, Fuller. Frank Garrison's out. Why would he kill the old woman? He had nothing to gain. Anyhow, I know him. He's a damned decent fellow."

"I've known—"

"All right. Who have you got? This young doc and Carlton Fairbanks. The doctor's out. So Carlton's left. Know him, too. Always thought he was a stuffed shirt."

"That wouldn't go far with a jury." Fuller smiled unhappily. "Anyhow, he doesn't seem to me the type. Of course—"

"Type? Type! Any type will kill for a half of three million dollars. That's what old Henry Fairbanks left his widow when he died. In bonds, Fuller! No hanky-panky, no cats and dogs, no common stocks. Bonds!"

"It sounds like a lot of money," said the inspector. "Maybe you'd like to talk to Fairbanks yourself."

The commissioner got up hastily. "Not at all," he said. "I've got an engagement. And I guess you have your own methods. Better than mine, probably!"

With that he departed, and the inspector felt that he was left virtually with a rubber hose in his hand.

Back at the Fairbanks house Hilda had not gone to bed. She took off her shoes and rubbed her tired feet, but she was not sleepy. The sense of failure was bitter in her. Yet what had she done? She had left the door to go up to the third floor, a matter of three minutes or so. She had been fifteen minutes, maybe twenty, in the kitchen, but the doctor had agreed to stand guard. And Mrs. Fairbanks had been alive then. She had turned on the radio after that, turned it on loudly, as if the movements in the hall outside the door had exasperated her.

What else? She had taken her tray back, and later on Susie had stepped in it. She had gone back and found her there. How long had that taken?

She got up, and to the astonishment of the officer in the hall, paced it off in her stocking feet, carrying her watch in her hand. She could hardly believe it when the second hand showed only a minute and a half. Then what? She and Susie had sat in the hall, until the slamming screen in Eileen's room had taken her in to it. Eileen had been asleep, and she had closed and hooked the screen. And after that she had found Mrs. Fairbanks dead, and her hands were already cool.

It was Carlton, then, after all. It had to be Carlton.

She went back to her room and stood looking out the window. Amos, in his best clothes and with a smug look on his face, was coming toward his Sunday dinner. Birds were busy on the grass after the rain the night before. The crowd outside had diminished somewhat as the meal hour arrived, but it was still there.

Carlton, she thought wretchedly. She could see him now, dressed in his striped trousers and black coat and wearing a mourning tie, trying to fill in the time with a hammer and an old cigar box filled with nails. Did men kill their mothers and then go puttering around fastening screens? Decent, quiet little men who liked the country and growing things?

The unreality grew when she sat at the midday dinner table, watching him carve a roast of beef into delicate slices.

"Well done or rare, Miss Adams?"

"Medium, please."

Not Carlton, she thought, looking around the table. Not any of them. Not Susie, in a black dress with little or no make-up, and for once not smoking. Not Jan. Oh, certainly not Jan, looking young and tragic and not eating. Not even young Brooke, watching Jan and making such talk as there was. Certainly not Eileen, sick and hysterical in her room upstairs. Not William, his head still shaking as he passed the food. Not Ida, pale but efficient. Not any of them, she thought drearily. Then who?

The guards were taken out of the house that afternoon, but Mrs. Fairbanks's room was left locked and sealed. There was still no news of Marian, and Jan, after a talk with her father on the telephone, had at last gone to bed and to sleep.

It was three o'clock in the afternoon when Carlton was taken to police headquarters for questioning.

Hilda was in the lower hall when it happened. He said nothing to anybody. When she saw him he was carefully selecting a stick from a stand, and he spoke to her quietly.

"If my wife asks for me," he said, "tell her I have some things to do downtown. I may be late, so ask her not to wait up for me."

She saw the car outside, with Captain Henderson and a detective waiting, and felt sorry for him, adjusting his hat in front of the mirror. When he turned she saw he was pale.

"I was fond of my mother, Miss Adams," he said strangely, and without looking back went out to the officers and the waiting car.

At four o'clock that same afternoon Marian Garrison came home.

17.

SHE ARRIVED apparently unwarned. Her first shock came when the taxi, violently honking its horn, tried to make its way through the crowd. The police officer drove it back, but when the driver stopped under the porte-cochere he found her collapsed in the seat and rang the doorbell.

"Lady here's in poor shape," he told William. "Want me to bring her in?"

William ran down the steps, to find her with her eyes shut and her face colorless.

"What is it? What's wrong, William?"

"I'm sorry, madam. Mrs. Fairbanks is dead."

"Dead? But the crowds! What's wrong? What happened to her?"

"It was quite painless. Or so they say. She was asleep when it took place. If—"

She reached out and caught him by the arm.

"Not poison, William? Not poison!"

He hesitated, his old head shaking violently.

"No, madam. I'm afraid— It was a knife."

She did not faint. She drew a long breath and got out of the car. The driver and William helped her into the house. But she could not walk far. She sat down on a chair inside the door snapping and unsnapping the fastening of her bag, her eyes on William.

"Who did it?" she asked, in a half-whisper.

"Nobody knows. Not yet. The police—"

She got up.

"I want to see Jan," she said wildly. "I must talk to her. I'd better try to go up to my room."

William caught her by the arm.

"Not right away, Miss Marian," he said in his quavering voice. "You see—"

She shook him off.

"What's the matter with you?" she demanded. "I'm going up to my room. Get Jan and tell her I'm here, and don't act the fool."

That was the situation when Jan ran down the stairs, Marian standing angry and bewildered, and William evidently at a loss to know what to do. She gave them one look and kissed her mother's cold face. But Marian did not return the caress.

"Why can't I go upstairs in my own home, Jan? What is all this?"

It was on this tableau that Hilda appeared, Marian's face flushed, Jan's pale, and her young body stiff.

"I'm sorry, Mother. We'll get her out as soon as we can. You see—"

"Get whom out?"

"Eileen. She's sick. She is in your room, Mother."

Marian's frail body stiffened.

"So that's it," she said. "You've brought her here and put her in my room. The woman who ruined my life, and you couldn't wait until I was gone to get her here!"

She would have gone on, but Hilda interfered. She took her into the library and gave her a stiff drink of Scotch. All the fire had gone out of her by that time. She seemed stunned. The liquor braced her, however, although she listened to Jan's story with closed eyes. But her first words when Jan finished her brief outline were addressed to Hilda.

"So you let it happen after all!" she said. "I left her in your care, and she was killed."

She was badly shaken, but she was frightened, too. Hilda was puzzled. She caught Marian watching Jan, as if the girl might know something she was not telling. She was more frightened than grieved, she thought. But she was coldly determined, too.

"Get that woman out of here," she said. "At once, Jan. Do you hear? If she can't walk, carry her. If she won't be carried, throw her out. And if none of you can do it I'll do it myself. Or strangle her," she added.

That was the situation when Hilda got the inspector on the telephone. He seemed annoyed, as though he resented the interruption, but he agreed to let Eileen go.

"She's hardly a suspect," he said. "Sure. Better get young Brooke's okay on it first."

She called the doctor, who agreed willingly, and went to Eileen's room. To her surprise Eileen was already out of bed and partly dressed. She was sitting in a chair while Ida drew on her stockings, and she was smiling coldly.

"I heard the fuss and rang," she said. "Tell them not to worry. I'm leaving. She can have her room. She can have the whole damned house, so far as I am concerned." She slid her feet into her pumps and stood up. "I suppose," she said, "that my loving husband has come back, too."

"He came back last night. From Washington."

Eileen looked at her sharply.

"From Washington? How do you know?"

"I saw him this morning."

"Where? Here?"

"I went to the apartment. Jan asked me to. He had been here last night and she was worried."

A flicker of alarm showed in Eileen's face.

"What do you mean, he was here? In the house?"

"In the grounds. He says he didn't know where you were, so he came and called up to Jan's window to find out."

Eileen sat down on the bed, as though her knees would not hold her.

"When—when was that?"

"Between one-thirty and two, I think," Hilda said.

"His plane got in at midnight, but he went home first. Then he walked here. It's quite a distance."

Eileen's face had turned a grayish color. She seemed to have difficulty in breathing.

"Do the police know that?" she asked, her lips stiff.

"They know he was in the grounds. He admits it himself." And then, because she was sorry for her, Hilda added, "I wouldn't worry too much about it, Mrs. Garrison. Of course, they're suspecting everybody just now. I'd better order a taxi. I can go with you if you like."

Eileen, however, wished for no company. When Hilda came back from the telephone she was looking better, or at least she was under control. She was in front of Marian's table, eyeing herself in the mirror. Almost defiantly she put on some rouge and lipstick, and finished her dressing. Ida had carried down her suitcase, and at the door she turned and surveyed the room.

"Did you ever know what it is to pray for somebody to die?" she said bitterly. "Did you ever see someone riding around in a car in the rain while you walked, and wish there would be an accident? Did you ever lie awake at night hating somebody so hard that you hit the pillow? Well, that's what Marian Garrison has done to me. And he still cares for her. After seven years he's still in love with her. He'd even go to the chair for her! The fool. The blind, stupid fool."

Carlton had not come home when Eileen left the house. He was still in the inspector's office, his dapper look gone, but his head still high.

"Just go over that again, Mr. Fairbanks. You went into the room, went around the foot of the bed, turned off the radio, and came directly out again. How could you see to turn off the radio? Did you light a match?"

"I didn't need to. It's an old one. We've had it for a long time. I knew where the switch was. And, of course, there was some light from the door into the hall."

"You still claim that you didn't speak to your mother?"

"I did not. She had a habit of going to sleep with the radio going. I've gone in and shut it off at times for the last ten years."

"You came out at once?"

"I did. Immediately. Ask the nurse. She was there."

But he was tired. He had eaten almost nothing that day, and although they gave him water when he asked for it and he was well supplied with cigarettes, he needed a drink badly. There was a cold sweat all over him and his mouth was dry. He moistened his lips.

"You had no reason, for instance, to investigate the closet where the safe is?"

"Why should I? It's been there for months."

"And the closet door?"

"Oh, for God's sake! How can I remember? What does it matter? Suppose it was open and I shoved it out of my way? What has that got to do with my mother's death?"

"Do you think anyone could have been hidden in the closet?"

"Who? My niece? My wife?"

"I'm asking the questions, Mr. Fairbanks," said the inspector. "You are the only person known to have entered your mother's room at or about the time she was—the time she died. I know this is painful, but we have to get on with it. If you had nothing to do with it you will want to be helpful. Nobody is trying to railroad you to the"—he coughed—"to jail. Now. You have said that you are one of the heirs to the estate."

A little of Carlton's dignity had returned. He was even slightly pompous.

"I presume so. My sister and myself. Probably there is something for my niece, Janice Garrison. I don't know, of course. My—my mother managed her own affairs."

"You must have some idea of the value of the estate."

But here he was on surer ground.

"It was a very large one at one time. Some values have shrunk, but it was carefully invested. Mostly in bonds."

"Did she keep those securities in the safe?"

"I don't know. I hope she didn't. She used to have several safe-deposit boxes at her bank. I suppose she still has them."

But always they went back to the night before. The knife. Had he seen it before? Had he bought it anywhere? Of course, knives and sales could be traced. He would understand that. And he didn't like the city, did he? He and his wife wanted a farm. Well, plenty of people wanted farms nowadays. He brightened over that.

"Certainly I wanted a farm," he said, his face brightening. "There's a living in it, if you work yourself. A man can keep his self-respect. I've studied it a good bit. These fellows who go out of town and play at it—they'll only lose their investments. They'll fix up the houses and build fancy chicken houses and pigpens, and in three or four years they'll be back in town again."

"The idea was to be independent of your mother, wasn't it?"

"Not entirely. But what if it was? There's nothing wrong about that."

They took him back, to the attempt to poison Mrs. Fairbanks on her return from Florida. He was indignant.

"I never believed she was poisoned. Not deliberately. Some kinds of food poisoning act the same way. I looked it up. She'd come back from Florida the day before. She might have eaten something on the train."

"The doctor doesn't think so."

"That young whippersnapper! What does he know?"

The inspector picked up a paper from his desk. "This is Doctor Brooke's statement," he said. He read: " 'Showed usual symptoms arsenical poisoning, heat and burning pain; was vomiting and very thirsty. When I saw her her pulse was feeble and she showed signs of collapse. Had severe cramps in legs. I gave her an emetic and washed out her stomach. Reinsch's test later showed arsenious acid, commonly known as white arsenic. I also found it in the sugar bowl on her tray. At request of family made no report to the police.' "

"Oh, my God!" said Carlton feebly.

He sat clutching the arms of his chair, hardly hearing what they asked him. He looked smaller than ever, as though he had been deflated, and his replies were almost monosyllabic.

"Do you know anything about this campaign to terrify your mother? The bats, I mean."

"No. Nothing."

"Nor how they were introduced into the room?"

"No."

"I'll ask that another way. Have you any suspicions as to how or why they were being used?"

And at that he blew up.

"No. No!" he shouted. "What are you trying to do to me? Make me confess to something I never did? I didn't poison my mother. I didn't kill her with a knife. I don't know anything about your damned animals. I don't know anybody cruel enough to—"

His voice broke. Tears rolled down his cheeks. He mopped at them helplessly with his handkerchief.

"I'm sorry, gentlemen," he said. "I didn't mean to make a fool of myself. I was up all night, and I haven't eaten anything today."

They gave him a little time. He lit a cigarette and tried to smile.

"All right," he said. "I guess I can take it now."

But they got nothing of importance from him, except a pretty thorough idea that he was keeping something back. They did not hold him, however. At eight o'clock that night the inspector drove him home. They stopped and had something to eat on the way, and Carlton drank two neat whiskies. He looked better when they reached the house.

There was no one in sight. Marian, after having her room

cleaned and aired, had retired to it and locked her door. Jan had gone with Courtney Brooke to see Eileen, and Hilda was packing her suitcase, preparatory to leaving, when she got the word. But Susie was waiting in the library. When she heard the car she flew out at the inspector like a wild creature.

"So you've had him!" she said. "The only one in this house who loved his mother, and you pick on him! If you've done anything to him you'll be sorry. Good and sorry."

"I'm all right, Susie," Carlton said mildly. But she was not to be placated.

"Why didn't you take that nurse of yours? Or Frank Garrison? Or me? I could have told you some of the things that have been going on."

"Oh, shut up, Susie," Carlton said wearily. "There's been too much talking as it is."

They were in the house by that time. He gave her a warning look, and she subsided quickly.

"What's been going on?" the inspector inquired.

"Marian's back, if that interests you. She raised hell until Eileen got out." She lit a cigarette and grinned at him. "Nice place we've got here," she said airily. "Come and stay sometime, if you ever get bored."

He left them downstairs, Susie mixing a highball and Carlton lighting a pipe. It would have been quite a nice domestic picture, he thought, if he had not known the circumstances.

Hilda was in her room when he went up the stairs. She was standing by her window, looking out, and her suitcase was packed and closed on a chair. He scowled at it.

"You're not leaving," he said. "I need you here."

"I have no patient."

"You'll stay if I have to break a leg. Get young Brooke to put the girl to bed. Nervous exhaustion. Anything, but you're staying." He looked at her. "Anything attractive outside that window?"

"No. I was just thinking."

"About what?"

She had assumed again her cherubic look, and he eyed her with suspicion. "Not much. Just a can of white paint."

"What?"

"A can of paint. Of course people do queer things when they're worried. They play solitaire, or bite their fingernails, or kick the dog. I knew one man who cut down a perfectly good tree while his wife was having a baby. But paint is different. It covers a lot of things."

"I see. Who's been painting around here?"

"Carlton Fairbanks. This morning. He nailed the screens shut and then painted over the marks he made."

"Very tidy," said the inspector.

"But he fastened his mother's screens weeks ago. I would like to know whether he painted them, too."

He laughed down at her indulgently.

"What you need is a night's sleep," he told her. "Go to bed and forget it. And remember, you're not leaving."

But she was stubborn. She wanted to see Mrs. Fairbanks's screens, and at last he unsealed and unlocked the door, and gave her the key. The room was as it had been left, the bedding thrown back, print powder showing here and there on the furniture. She went straight to a window.

"You see, he didn't."

"I'm damned if I know why that's important."

"I don't know myself. Not yet."

"All right. Go to it," he told her, still indulgent, and left her there, a small intent figure in the ghostly room, still gazing at the screens.

He yawned as he got into his car. The crowd outside the fence had practically disappeared. Only a scant half-dozen men still stood there, the die-hards who would not give up until all hope of further excitement was over. He did not notice them. What on earth had Hilda meant about white paint? What had white paint to do with the murder? The thing nagged him all the way back to his office and later on even to his bed.

Back in Mrs. Fairbanks's room Hilda switched off the lights and prepared to leave. She knew death too well to be afraid, but the impress of Mrs. Fairbanks's small old body on the bed had revived her sense of failure. She stood still. What could she have done? What had she failed to do?

And then she heard it again, a faint scuffling noise from the closet.

18.

SHE JERKED the door open, but the closet was empty. The shoe bag still hung on the door, the safe was closed, and the sounds had ceased. Save for the low remote voice of Carlton and Susie from the library below the house was silent.

Out in the hall she felt better. The noise, whatever it was, had not been what she had heard before, and turning briskly she opened the door of Carlton's room and went in. She stopped abruptly.

There was a man in the closet. He was standing with his back to her, and fumbling among the clothes hanging there.

She felt for the light switch and turned it on, to see William emerging, blinking.

"Is anything wrong, miss?" he asked.

She was surprised to discover that she was trembling.

"No. I was in Mrs. Fairbanks's room and I heard a noise. I thought—"

He smiled, showing his excellent set of false teeth.

"It was me in the closet," he explained. "I look after Mr. Carl's clothes. He wants a suit pressed, and he's got paint on the toes of these shoes this morning. I'm sorry if I scared you. I am afraid we are all in a bad state of nerves. If you'll excuse me—"

She felt exceedingly foolish as he passed her with his usual impeccable dignity, but in doing so he dropped one of the shoes. She picked it up and looked at it. It was an old tan one, with a smear of white paint across the toe, and the ones Carlton had worn that morning had been black. There could be no doubt of it. She could see him now, his black shoes, his morning coat and striped trousers, as he moved from room to room, carrying his cigar box and hammer, and later the small can of white paint.

William had not noticed. He thanked her and went out, and she turned off the light behind him. She did not go out, however. She stood still until she heard him going down the back stairs. Then she closed the door, fumbled for a box of matches and getting down on her knees, began systematically to examine the row of neatly treed shoes on the closet floor.

She did not hear the door opening behind her. Only when the light went on did she realize that Carlton had come into the room. She turned, still on her knees, the smoldering match in her hand, to see him coming at her, his face contorted, the veins on his forehead swollen with fury.

For a moment she thought he was going to attack her. She got up quickly.

"I'm sorry," she said. "I was in your mother's room, and I heard a noise in here. I thought it might be another rat."

He did not believe her. She saw that. He took a step or two toward her and stopped.

"Aren't you through here? In this house?" he said, his voice thick with anger. "My mother doesn't need you anymore. Eileen Garrison has gone. Are you supposed to stay indefinitely, snooping around about what doesn't concern you?"

"Are you so sure it doesn't concern me?" she inquired. "The police sent me here, at your mother's request. And they haven't released me yet. I assure you I am more than willing to go."

He got himself under control with difficulty. He walked past her and closed the closet door. When he faced her again his voice was more normal.

"At least I can ask you to keep out of the family rooms," he said. "There are no rats in the house, and if anything of this sort happens again I advise you to notify the servants."

She left with such dignity as she could muster. As she opened the door of her room she heard again the soft slithering sound she had heard before, but she was too shaken to investigate it. She stood at her window for some time, trying to think. It was very black outside. With the disappearance of the crowd the guards had evidently been removed, for by the light of the lamp on Huston Street she could see no one there. The stable was dark, as though Amos was either out or asleep.

She was astonished when the luminous dial of her watch showed only ten o'clock.

She was still there a few minutes later when Marian rapped at her door and slipped inside.

"Don't turn on the light," she said. "It's too hot. Miss Adams, you were here. You saw it all. Who did it? Who killed my mother?"

Hilda could not see her. She was only a vague figure in the room, but her voice was hard and strained.

"I wish I knew, Mrs. Garrison."

"That woman—why did she come here?"

"I think Mrs. Fairbanks had told her—"

"Nonsense," Marian said sharply. "She had some purpose of her own. That statement that Frank was with me! I suppose she was after money. Did Mother give her any?"

"I wasn't in the room. She may have."

Marian took a case from the pocket of her housecoat and lit a cigarette. In the light from the match she looked more haggard than ever, but it was Jan's eyes, dark and tragic, that looked out from her raddled face.

"I don't understand anything," she said. "Why did they put her in my room? The whole third floor was empty. And why have the police taken the screen from one of my windows? They have it, haven't they?"

"There is a chance somebody got into the house last night through that window," Hilda said guardedly. "I found it open. It could have been done from the roof of the porte-cochere. It was only a hook, and the blade of a knife— Or, of course, it might have been opened from within, by someone in the room."

Marian dropped her cigarette.

"Oh, God!" she said. "Frank, of course. They think it was Frank, and she let him in! Have they arrested him yet?"

"No. They've talked to him. That's all."

"They will arrest him," she said in a flat voice. "Jan says he was outside. They will arrest him, and what defense has he? He could have climbed to the roof. He's very strong. I've seen him do it, on a bet. They'll say she let him into her room and hid him there. But he didn't do it, Miss Adams. He cared for my mother. He was the kindest man on earth. He's had the patience of God himself, and I ruined his life. I was a jealous fool. I let him go. I made him go. So now—"

Hilda let her talk. Mentally she was back at the window of

Marian's room the night before, and something was whipping about in the wind outside. She looked at Marian.

"When I closed the screen in your room last night, before I found your mother, there was a light rope fastened to one of the outside shutters. Do you know anything about it?"

"A rope? Something that could be climbed? Good heavens, are you trying to say that Frank—"

"It wasn't strong enough for that. Or long enough. I just wondered about it."

But Marian was vague.

"I wouldn't know," she said. "It might have been there for years. I don't remember it."

Hilda went back with her to her room. It had changed, she thought, since Eileen was in it. The bed had a silk cover and small bright-colored pillows. The dressing-table where Eileen had so defiantly made up her face only a few hours ago still had the gold toilet set, but it was crowded now with creams and perfumes. A silver fox scarf had been tossed on a chair, and sheer undergarments, unpacked but not put away, lay on the chaise longue.

"Ida wasn't well," Marian said indifferently. "I sent her to bed."

She had apparently forgotten the rope. But Hilda looked for it, raising the window to do so. It was gone. Marian shrugged when she told her.

"Maybe you only imagined it."

"I didn't imagine it," said Hilda dryly.

Back in her room she tried to fit the pieces of the puzzle together, but she got nowhere. The rope had been there. Now it was gone. It must be important, must mean something. Had Eileen taken it away, and if so why? Or had someone in the house removed it? Not Carlton. He had been away after Eileen left and Marian arrived. Not Jan. She had gone to see Eileen and had not come back. Susie? She was quite capable of it, if it was important. She would have no scruples, Susie. But why would it be important? A rope and a bit of white paint on a tan shoe. They must fit somehow. Or did they?

She felt the need of action. For days, she thought, things had been going on around her. Not only the murder; small stealthy movements, doors opening and closing, people talking and saying nothing, going out and coming in, and always she had been merely the watcher, seeing but not comprehending. The night Carlton had carried the bundle from the stable, the figure at the top of the stairs, the open screen in Eileen's room, and now—of all silly things—a missing rope.

She looked across. Susie's light was on. It showed over the transom, and she went over and knocked lightly at the door. But she did not go into the room. Standing there she could hear Susie crying, childish sobs that were as unrestrained as everything else about her.

She got her flashlight from her suitcase and went down the stairs. The doctor's car had just driven in. There was no mistaking its rattle, or the cough of its ancient engine. Young Brooke did not come into the house, however. Jan opened the door and stood there, her voice cool.

"I don't understand you. That's all," she said.

"I've told you. I'm not living off any woman. You're going to have money now, and I'm peculiar about money." His voice was stubborn. "I'll support my own wife, or I won't have one."

"I wouldn't use the money, Court."

"There's where you're wrong, my darling. You think you wouldn't. You think you'd go hungry and without shoes. You wouldn't. I watched you this afternoon and tonight, cleaning up the mess at your stepmother's. You didn't like it, did you? And that's luxury, my child. One week of boiled beef and cabbage—"

"You can't see anything but your perfectly sickening pride, can you?" said Jan, and closed the door on him.

Hilda went back to the kitchen. Unless the police had taken the rope it must be somewhere in the house, or in the yard. She tried the trash cans and the garbage pails outside without result. Then rather reluctantly she went down to the basement. It was enormous. She did not like to turn on the lights, and her flash made only a small pool of illumination in the darkness. There was rope there, a large coil of it for some reason in a preserve closet, but it was thick and heavy.

When she did find it it was in the furnace. A small fire had been built around it at some time, but it was only charred, not consumed. She pulled it out and turned the light on it, some eight feet of thin blackened rope, which must be important since someone had attempted to destroy it. She went back over the night before when she had seen it, Eileen asleep in her bed, the pouring rain, the slapping screen. And Susie in the hall, drenched to the skin.

She felt the ashes in the furnace. They were still faintly warm. Quite recently, then—within two or three hours—someone had tried to destroy it. She tried to think what it meant, but she was tired. She had slept a little that afternoon and since then she had been going around in circles.

Nobody saw her as she carried it upstairs. She wrapped it in a piece of newspaper and laid it in the top of her suitcase. Maybe tomorrow her mind would be clearer, or the inspector would fit it into his puzzle. All she wanted now was to go to bed.

She undressed by the open window, for the sake of the breeze. That was how she happened to see Jan when she left the house. Even in the darkness there was no mistaking her slim figure, the easy grace with which she moved. On her way to Courtney Brooke, she thought comfortably. To make it up, to say she was sorry, to effect a compromise between his pride and her own. Then she stared. Jan was not crossing Huston Street. There was no sign of her under the street light. She had gone into the stable.

Hilda never quite understood the fear which made her snatch up a dressing-gown and her flashlight and follow her. The lights were out in the lower hall, but the door to the porte-cochere was open. She was in her bare feet as she ran across the grass. Once at the stable, however, she began to feel foolish. The doors to the garage were closed and Amos's windows overhead were dark. There was no sound to be heard, and it was not until she turned on her light that she saw the door to the staircase standing open. She stepped inside and looked up. It seemed to her that there was a small flickering light above in the loft.

Then it came, a crash from overhead that sounded as though the roof had fallen in. She was too shocked to move at first. She stood still, staring up. Her voice when it came sounded thin and cracked.

"Jan!" she called. "Jan! Are you there?"

There was no answer, and she ran up the stairs. At the top she turned the flashlight into the loft.

Jan was lying without moving on the floor, blood streaming from a cut on her forehead, and the heavy ladder was lying beside her.

19.

SHE WAS not dead. That was the first thing Hilda ascertained. Her pulse was rapid but strong, and she was breathing regularly; and Hilda's heart, which had been trying to choke her, settled back into its proper place. The cause of the accident seemed obvious. For some reason Jan had used the ladder to reach the cupola, and it had slipped. The cut was from an old birdcage on the floor beside her.

Hilda's first impulse was to go to the house for help. Amos was evidently out. His door was standing open and his rooms dark. But she felt an odd reluctance to leaving the girl there alone. She made her way across the small landing into Amos's rooms and turning on the lights, found the bathroom. There she got a clean towel and a basin of water, and was turning back when she heard the far door quietly closing.

At first she thought it had closed itself. She put down the basin and towel and pulled at it. It did not yield, however, and at last she realized that it was locked. Someone had reached in while the water was running, taken out the key and locked it from the outside.

Hilda was frantic. She beat on the door, but there was only silence beyond. Then her practical, rational mind began to assert itself. She opened a window and looked out. There was no one in sight save a woman whistling for a dog across Huston Street, and the distance was too great for her to drop. But there must be some method of communication with the house. She looked about, and found a house telephone beside Amos's bed. Even then she was not too hopeful. It probably rang in the kitchen or back hall, and the household was upstairs. To her relief, however, it was answered almost at once.

Carlton's voice, sounding resentful, came over the wire.

"What the hell's the matter, Amos?" he said. "Place on fire?"

"It's Hilda Adams, Mr. Fairbanks," she told him. "Jan's had an accident in the stable loft, and I'm locked in."

His reaction was slow.

"What do you mean, you're locked in?"

"Someone has locked me in Amos's rooms. And Jan's hurt. She's in the loft. I don't know what's happening, but hurry. I—"

He did not wait for her to finish. From the window she saw him emerge from the house and come running across the lawn, his dressing-gown flapping around his legs. She stood inside the door as he climbed the stairs, but he went on to the loft. There was a brief silence, while he scratched a match or two. Then his voice, outside the door.

"She must have fallen," he said. "I'll get Brooke."

"Don't leave her there," she said. "Not alone. I don't think she fell. There's someone around, Mr. Fairbanks. She's not badly hurt. Not yet anyhow. But don't leave her."

"What on earth am I to do?"

"Look around for the key. It may be out there, or on the stairs."

He found it finally. It had been dropped just outside the door. But he had used his last match. When Hilda emerged it was into darkness, and the loft also was dark.

"My flashlight," she said. "I left it here."

"No light when I got here. See if Amos has a candle, or matches. I'll get the doctor."

She felt her way to Jan. She was still unconscious, but when Hilda touched her she moved slightly. She sat down on the floor beside her in the dark, and she was still there when Carlton came back, bringing Courtney Brooke with him.

After that there was a good bit of confusion. The two men carried Jan to the house, the family was roused, and Susie, to everybody's discomfiture, went into violent hysterics. Hilda gave her a good whiff of household ammonia and Susie, choking for breath, came out of it. She looked up, tears streaming from her eyes.

"It's my fault," she said. "I knew I ought to tell. But Carl—"

"What should you have told?"

Susie did not say. She closed her eyes and went into a stubborn silence.

Across the hall Courtney was sitting beside Jan's bed, holding an ice pack to her head. Instead of a shirt he wore the coat of his pajamas, and his face was grim.

"Someone tried to kill her," he said. "She fell first. Then she was struck with the flashlight. There is blood on it."

Marian stared at him from across the bed, her face filled with horror.

"But who would do that to her?" she demanded. "Who would want to kill her?" She leaned over the bed. "Jan. Jan! Who hurt you? What happened to you?"

"I'd let her alone," he said. "She is coming out of it. The quieter she is the better. She'll be all right, Mrs. Garrison."

At midnight Frank Garrison arrived. Carlton, telephoning wildly, had finally located him at his club. He came into the room, his tall figure seeming to fill it, and Marian went pale when she saw him.

"What are *you* doing here?"

"She is my child, Marian," he said politely.

"You deserted her. You deserted us both."

He ignored that. He asked about Jan, and Courtney gave him his place beside the bed. Marian got up, her face a tortured mask.

"You are driving me out of this room. You know that, don't you? Why don't you go back to your woman? Jan is nothing to you. Less than nothing."

"Sit down, Marian," he said gravely. "This is our girl. We have at least that in common. And be quiet. I think she is coming out of it."

But Jan, coming out of it, was not much help. After her first wondering gaze around the room she simply said that her head ached, and after that she went to sleep. She was still sleeping when at three in the morning her father left the house, and the doctor sent Hilda to bed.

"She's all right," he said. "She'll have a day or two in bed, but that's all. You'd better get some sleep. You look as though you need it. I'm staying anyhow."

She slept for three hours. Then she got up and put on her uniform. In Jan's room Courtney Brooke was asleep, as was Jan herself, and she went downstairs and let herself out without disturbing anyone.

At the stable Amos had returned. Even before she climbed

the stairs she heard him snoring. A dim light from the cupola showed her the loft as they had left it; the ladder lying across the floor, the trunks, the broken furniture. But lying where Jan's body had fallen was something she had not noticed the night before, a large piece of unbleached muslin some four feet square. She picked it up and examined it. It looked fairly new, and it had certainly not been there when Amos showed her the loft some days before.

She put it down and was stooping over the ladder when Amos appeared. He had pulled a pair of trousers over his night-shirt, and he was in a bad humor.

"What are you doing here?" he asked suspiciously. "If a man works all day and can't get his proper sleep—"

She cut him short.

"Lift this ladder, Amos. I want to look at the cupola."

"What for?"

"That's my business. Miss Jan was hurt here last night. I want to know why."

"Hurt? Not bad, is it?"

"Bad enough. She'll get over it."

The cupola, however, revealed nothing at first. It was floored, save for the square opening for the ladder. Such light as there was was admitted by slotted openings on the four sides. Except that in one place the dust of ages seemed to have been disturbed, it appeared empty. Then she saw something; an old pair of chauffeur's gloves. They had been shoved back into a corner, but she managed to reach them. She showed them to Amos when she climbed down again.

"Are these yours?"

He stared at them. Then he grinned.

"So that's where they went!" he said.

"You didn't put them up there?"

"Why would I put them up there?" he demanded truculently. "I lost them two or three months ago. I thought somebody stole them."

He wanted them back, but Hilda to his fury took them back to the house with her. One part of the mystery, she felt, was solved. But before she left she turned to him.

"I suppose you can account for your own movements last night?"

He took a step toward her, looking ugly.

"So I hurt her, did I?" he said harshly. "Like my own daughter, and I try to kill her! Sure I can account for where I was last night, if that's any of your business. You don't have to come out to the stable to find your murderer, Miss Police Nurse. Look in the house."

Jan was better that morning. Outside of a headache and some bruises she had suffered no ill effects. She even drank a cup of coffee and ate a piece of toast. But she had no idea what had happened to her, except that she thought the ladder had slipped.

She had not gone to bed. She had quarreled with Courtney and she could not sleep. She had decided to go over and see him. She had reached the stable when she heard a sound overhead. She thought it was Amos, and called to tell him that the door to the staircase was open. Amos, however, had not answered, so she had climbed the stairs.

She was not frightened. She had thought for some time that the bats in her grandmother's room might have come from the cupola.

"There were slits in the shutters," she said. "Pigeons couldn't get in, but bats might."

What she thought she heard, she said, might have been bats flying around. No, she couldn't describe it. It was just a sound. Not very loud, either. She knew the loft well. She had played there as a child. She didn't even light a match until she got there.

To her surprise the ladder was in place. She decided to investigate the cupola, and striking a match she climbed it. She was near the top when it gave way under her.

"I felt it going," she said. "I couldn't catch anything. I—well, I guess I just fell. I don't remember."

They let her think that. She was not told that it had probably been jerked from under her, or of the savage attack on her with the flashlight.

Hilda saw the inspector later that morning, sitting across from him, and placing on the desk between them the piece of muslin, the gloves, a small can of white paint, and the piece of charred rope. Fuller eyed them solemnly.

"You're slipping," he said. "No snakes? No guinea pigs?"

He looked tired. He had slept badly, and it almost annoyed him to see Hilda, bland and fresh, her hands neatly folded in her lap.

"You're not human," he said. "And what in God's name does all this stuff mean?"

"Somebody tried to kill Janice Garrison last night."

He almost leaped out of his chair.

"What?" he yelled. "And you didn't call me? See here. I'll be damned if I'll have you running this case. You've let one murder happen, and now you tell me—"

He choked, and Hilda looked more bland than ever.

"I thought you needed your sleep," she said calmly. "And the family didn't want you." She smiled faintly. "They said they had had enough of you to last a long time."

"Who said that?"

"I think it was Carlton."

She told her story after that, the attack on Jan, her own discovery of the girl, being locked in Amos's rooms, and Carlton coming to the rescue.

"So he was downstairs, was he?"

"He was. Probably getting a drink."

Fuller leaned back in his chair.

"You don't think he is guilty, do you?"

"I think he was fond of his mother."

Their eyes clashed, the inspector's hard, Hilda's blue and childlike, and stubborn.

"He had the motive and the opportunity."

"You couldn't get an indictment on that, could you? No grand jury—"

"All right," he said resignedly. "Now what's all this stuff?"

Hilda smiled.

"I don't know about the rope. Not yet, anyhow. But suppose you wanted to scare an old lady, maybe bring on a heart attack. And suppose she's afraid of bats. Other things, too, like rats. You might get a supply of them, put them in an old birdcage covered with a piece of muslin and hide them where nobody ever went."

"The cupola?"

"The cupola. But bats—and other things—have teeth. At least I think so. So you use a pair of heavy gloves. You might look at those gloves. They have small holes in them."

"Where would you get the bats—and so forth?"

"Out of the cupola itself. I didn't see any. I probably scared them away. But there's a butterfly net in the loft. I suppose it would be possible."

He threw up his hands.

"All right. You win," he said. "But how did they get into the room?"

"I imagine that's where the paint comes in," she said tranquilly.

She was there for some time. When she got up the inspector went to the door with her. Always she amused him, often she delighted him, but that morning there was a new look of admiration in his eyes.

"You're a highly useful person, Miss Pinkerton," he said, smiling down at her. "If I didn't think you'd slap me I'd kiss you."

"It wouldn't be the first time."

"Which?" he said quizzically. "Slap or kiss?"

"Both," she said, and went out.

Ida was dusting the lower hall when she went back. She did not look up, and Hilda did not speak to her. She had no idea that it was to be the last time she was to see the girl alive.

20.

THE INQUEST was held at two o'clock that afternoon. It was very brief. Carlton Fairbanks identified his mother's body, and nothing new was developed. Susie came home looking sick and went to bed, but Marian stayed downtown to make arrangements for the funeral and to buy the conventional black.

She was still out when the inspector arrived at four that afternoon. Jan was better, sitting up in bed, with Courtney Brooke in and out of the room, but mostly in. They did not talk much. It seemed to content them merely to be together. And Carlton was in the library. He had had a drink or two, but he was entirely sober.

He did not seem surprised to see the inspector. He stood up stiffly.

"I rather expected you," he said. "Jan's accident, and all that. But I want to ask you not to judge us on what may seem unusual. If any one of us has been at fault—"

Here, however, his voice failed him. It was a moment or so before he pulled himself together.

"I know things look bad," he said. "When I saw the paint was gone— But it has nothing to do with my mother's death. Nothing. I am innocent, and so—God help her—is my wife."

He followed the inspector up the stairs. Hilda, watching them come, thought he would not make the top. He rallied, however, when she unlocked the door of the death room, although he did not look at the bed.

The inspector was brisk and businesslike. He went at once to the closet and ignoring the safe got down on his knees and examined the baseboard. He used a flashlight, and he rapped on it and listened, his head on one side, while Carlton stood mutely by. When he got up his voice was brisk.

"All right," he said. "Now I'd like to see your room, please."

This time Carlton led the way. He looked shrunken, incredibly aged. Once inside he closed the door to Susie's room, but when the inspector opened his closet door he spoke for the first time.

"I give you my word of honor," he said bleakly, "that I knew nothing about this until yesterday morning. I would have told you before, but it involved"—he swallowed—"it involved someone very dear to me."

He said nothing more. He stood silent while the inspector took out the row of neatly treed shoes. Even the tan ones were there, although the paint had been removed. The inspector picked up his flashlight and turned it on the baseboard.

"How does this open?"

"It slides—toward the fireplace. It's nailed now."

"Since yesterday?"

"Since yesterday. I nailed and painted it yesterday morning."

The white paint was dry. The inspector produced from his pocket one of those small arrangements where a number of tools are carried inside the handle. He fitted one and went to work. Carlton said nothing. A breeze from the open windows blew the curtains into the room. Outside the traffic of a busy Monday moved along the streets, and Joe's Market was filled with women, shopping and gossiping.

"That police car's back. Look, you can see it."

"Much good it will do. They don't arrest people like the Fairbankses for murder."

It took some time to slide the panel. The paint held it. But at last it moved and the inspector picked up his flashlight. He saw a small empty chamber, the thickness of the wall, and beyond it a flat wooden surface fastened to the floor with hooks and screweyes. He opened it, and saw as he had expected; that it was the baseboard of Mrs. Fairbanks's closet. On his right was the safe. He could touch it, but he could not reach the dial. The whole aperture was only seven inches high.

He got up, dusting his hand.

"I suppose that accounts for a number of things," he said. "Not only for the attempts to frighten your mother. It could account for something else, Mr. Fairbanks."

"For what?"

"A cable for a remote control to the radio in your mother's room. I suggest that your mother was killed earlier in the night, that you turned on the radio from here, that you later re-entered the room ostensibly to shut it off, but actually to disconnect the cable, and that when you went to the closet it was to place the cable there, so you could withdraw it quietly from this side."

"Before God I never did."

That was when Susie burst into the room. She came like fury, ready to spring at Fuller.

"You fool!" she said. "You stupid fool! He never knew about it until yesterday."

Carlton roused at that.

"Be still," he said. "Don't make things worse. They're bad enough. Go back to your room. I'll—"

She paid no attention to him. She was panting with anger and fear.

"Don't listen to him. I did it. I had it done. He'd never have found it if I'd had a chance to close it all the way. But if you think I put those creatures in his mother's room, I didn't." Her voice was shrill. She was trembling. "Someone else in this house did that. Not me. I wouldn't touch them with a ten-foot pole."

She came out with her story. Nothing would have stopped her. Carlton had turned his back and was staring out the window. The inspector listened. Hilda watched.

It had started the winter before, she said. She had been in the bank, and she had seen Mrs. Fairbanks receive a large bundle of currency.

"She didn't see me," she said. "I saw her go down to her safe-deposit box, and I knew she was hoarding money. I told Carl, but he didn't believe me. Anyhow, he said it was his mother's business."

Then came the matter of the safe. Why did she want a safe in her room? And she had changed in other ways, too. She became stingy with money. She had sent away the kitchenmaid and the second housemaid.

"I was scared," Susie said. "I knew damned well why she wanted a safe in her room. Maybe I was raised on the wrong side of the tracks, but I had a pretty good idea what she was doing; selling her securities and turning them into cash to save taxes. And now she was going to keep it in the house!

"I got my brother-in-law the job of doing the carpentry

work," she said defiantly. "The safe was to be built into the wall, and I told him what I thought. Suppose she had two or three million dollars in cash in this house? A lot of people might know, her banks, her brokers. Things like that leak out. It wasn't safe. *We* weren't safe. Even if there was a fire—"

Her brother-in-law had suggested that she could at least keep an eye on things. "You can't change her," he said, "but you can watch her. Then if she's doing it you can get that son of hers to work on her. If she's trying to escape her taxes she ought to go to jail."

Mrs. Fairbanks and Marian were in Florida, Jan was visiting a school friend, and she and Carl were out of town for days at a time looking for a farm. He had no difficulty in doing the work. And when the old lady came back she—Susie—learned a good bit. Mostly by listening. Mrs. Fairbanks would drive out, come back and put something in the safe. After a time, as the money apparently accumulated, she developed a new habit. She would lock her door at night, set up a card table, and apparently count over her hoard.

"I didn't dare to open the baseboard all the way," Susie said, "but I'd push it out an inch or so. She kept her shoes in a shoe bag on the door, so they didn't bother me. She'd pretend to be playing solitaire, but she didn't fool me! But when I tried to tell Carl he wouldn't believe it. I didn't dare to tell him how I knew."

As to a possible cable to the radio and a remote control, she dismissed that with a gesture.

"That's crazy," she said. "He never knew the thing was there until after his mother was dead and he hunted out some black shoes yesterday morning to wear with his morning coat. Then he gave me hell, and yesterday he nailed it up." She went over and put a hand on Carlton's arm. "The one thing he suspected me of I didn't do," she said softly. "He thought I was keeping the bats in the stable. He found a birdcage up there wrapped in a cloth, and he was bringing it to me when the nurse saw him. He had to take it back!"

She eyed Hilda without rancor.

"You're pretty smart," she said, "but you missed that, didn't you? That's why I went out there in the rain that night. Carl had told me about it, and I wanted to see if it was still there, and what was in it."

"But you never got there?"

"I was scared off," said Susie, suddenly wary. "Somebody grabbed me. I don't know who."

Down in the kitchen Maggie was looking at the clock.

"I'd like to know what's keeping Ida," she observed. "She said she'd be gone only an hour, and it's five now." She poured William a cup of tea and took one for herself. "She's been queer lately," she said. "Ever since the old lady's death, and before."

"She'll be all right," said William. "Maybe she went to a movie."

But no one upstairs was thinking of Ida. Not then, certainly. Carlton did not know the combination to his mother's safe, and the inspector was anxious to open it.

"I think she would have written it down," Carlton said worriedly. "Her memory wasn't very good lately. Perhaps you have seen it, Miss Adams. It would be a combination of some sort, I suppose. Letters and numbers."

Hilda, however, had seen nothing of the sort. She had never seen Mrs. Fairbanks open the safe, and in the search of her room which followed nothing developed. They took the pictures from the walls, raised the rug at its edges, looked through the bed and under the paper lining the drawers of her table and bureau. They even examined the few books lying about, the vases on the mantel, the back of the clock and the radio, as well as the cards with which—according to Susie—she had merely pretended to play solitaire.

They were almost friendly, the four of them, during that interval. At least a common cause united them. When Maggie came to the door at a quarter to six, it was to see Mrs. Fairbanks's room completely dismantled, Susie on a chair examining the top of the draperies at the window, and an inspector of police lying under the bed, with only his legs protruding.

She looked apologetic.

"I didn't mean to disturb anybody," she said, highly embarrassed. "It's about Ida. She went out at one o'clock for an hour or so, and she hasn't come back yet."

The inspector had crawled out. He stood up and dusted his clothes.

"Does she often do that?"

"Never before, to my knowledge."

"Did she say where she was going?"

"She said she needed some darning silk. I wanted her to eat her lunch first. She looked sick. But she wouldn't wait."

The inspector looked at his watch.

"It's almost six now. Five hours. I wouldn't worry. She'll probably show up."

Ida did not show up, however. Marian came home from her shopping and her interview with the mortician looking exhausted and, refusing dinner, lay on her chaise longue, her eyes closed and her face bitter.

Carlton was closeted with Susie in her room, and Jan and Courtney had a double tray on the side of her bed, achieving the impossible of balancing it, holding hands, and still doing away with a considerable amount of food.

When Hilda carried it out he followed her.

"See here," he said. "What's been going on? What's this about Ida being missing?"

"I don't know that she is, doctor."

"Well, what's the row about? Maggie says you've practically torn up the old lady's room."

"We've been trying to locate the combination of her safe."

He whistled and looked back at Jan's door.

"I wouldn't tell her that, Miss Adams," he said. "It might upset her."

He declined to elaborate, and Hilda had that to puzzle over during the evening, as well as Ida's continued absence. At eight o'clock William had sent a wire to her people in the country, and he and Maggie were waiting in the kitchen for an answer. Young Brooke, having eaten his dinner, left for his office hours and came back at nine. Marian went to bed, and Carlton and Susie were in the library. Hilda, not needed anywhere, sat in her room and watched the twilight turn into night. She had gathered up a lot of odds and ends, but where did they take her? She was no nearer the solution of the crime than she had been before.

Ida? What about Ida? She could have discovered the opening into Mrs. Fairbanks's room; the panel not entirely closed, and Ida on her knees, washing the floor of the closet. She could even have slipped the bats into the room. She had been a country girl. She would not be afraid of such things. But why? What would be her motive?

She went back to the morning of the murder; Ida in her room by the window, her hands folded in her lap and a queer look on her long thin face as she and the inspector entered. She had been afraid, so afraid that she tried to rise and could not. And now she was missing.

In the next room the young people were talking. Hilda got up and moving carefully went to the front hall. Above her the third floor loomed dark and empty, and the long passage to Ida's room was ghostly. As the evening cooled the old house creaked, and Hilda, remembering the figure she had seen at the top of the stairs, felt small goose pimples on her flesh.

Once back in the girl's room, however, she felt better. She turned on the light and looked about her. There was no indication that she had intended to leave. A pair of washed stockings hung over the back of a chair, a discarded blue uniform lay on the bed, and a battered suitcase stood on the closet floor.

The wastebasket was empty, except for a newspaper, but under the pine dresser she found a scrap of paper. It was part of a letter, and it contained only two words. On one line was the word "sorry" and below it "harmless." Nowhere could she find any other bits, and at last she gave it up and put out the light.

She went quietly forward and down to the second floor. To her surprise the door into Mrs. Fairbanks's room was open, and she stepped inside. Young Brooke was there. He had opened the drawer of the table and had taken something out.

He started violently when he saw her. Then he grinned.

"Looking for cards," he said. "Jan and I want to play some gin-rummy."

He showed her the cards, but Hilda held out her hand for them.

"I'll take those," she said. "My orders are that nothing is to leave this room."

"Oh, have a heart. A pack of cards—"

"Give them to me, please. There are cards downstairs."

He gave them up reluctantly.

"And what will you do with them?" he inquired.

"Put them back where they belong," she said stiffly, "and lock this door."

She waited until he had gone out. Then she locked the door and took the key.

At midnight the telegram came. Ida had not gone home. And Hilda, getting Marian some hot milk to enable her to sleep, found the servants still there, Maggie and William and, smoking a pipe by the door, Amos. They were, she thought, both worried and watchful. And Maggie was convinced that Ida was dead.

"She was a good girl," she said tearfully. "A good Christian, too. And she minded her own business."

Amos shook the ashes out of his pipe.

"Did she now?" he said. "Sure of that, are you? Then what was she doing in my place yesterday, after the old lady was killed?"

"You're making that up."

"Am I? I found her in my bedroom, looking out of the window. She was a snooper. That's what she was. I never did trust her."

"You never trusted anybody," said Maggie scornfully. "What would she want in your room anyhow?"

"That's what I asked her. She said she had brought me some blankets. I've been here thirty years and she's been here ten. It's the first time she's been interested in my bed."

He seemed to think that was humorous. He grinned, but Maggie eyed him disdainfully.

"You might at least be grateful."

"Grateful? For blankets at the beginning of summer? Them blankets were an excuse to get in my room, and don't tell me different."

That night Hilda discovered why Susie had fainted a few days before.

Jan had sent her to bed, and she went gladly enough. All she wanted, she thought, was a hot bath and sleep, and tomorrow she could go home, to her bird and her sunny sitting-room. She had done all she could. She had not solved the murder, but she had solved one mystery. She locked the bit of paper from Ida's room in her suitcase, got out a fresh nightgown, and after some hesitation put the key to Mrs. Fairbanks's room under her pillow. Then she undressed and reached into the closet for her bedroom slippers. Curled up in one of them was something cold and clammy, and as she touched it it slithered out across her feet and under the bed.

She was too paralyzed to move for a moment. Then she put on her slippers and going across the hall rapped at Susie's door. Susie was in bed, the usual cigarette in one hand, the usual lurid magazine in the other.

"You might tell Mr. Fairbanks," Hilda said coldly, "that the thing that scared you into a faint the other night is under my bed. I believe it's harmless."

"Harmless!" Susie said. "I put my hand on it in that damned peephole, and it nearly scared me to death. It's a—"

"Yes," said Hilda calmly. "It's a snake. It would be nice to know who put it there."

21.

OFFICE OF CHIEF MEDICAL EXAMINER
REPORT OF DEATH

Name of deceased: *Unknown*
Last residence: *Unknown*
Date and time of death: *June 17, 1941. One a.m.*
Date and time examiner notified: *June 17, 1941. Two a.m.*
Body examined: *June 17, 1941. Eight a.m.*
Reported by: *City Hospital*
Body found: *At Morgue*
Pronounced dead by: *Dr. Cassidy*
Sex: *Female*
Age: *Approximately 40*
Color: *White*
    Notes:
    Woman reported discovered in great pain in rest room of Stern & Jones department store at 4 p.m. Store physician called and gave treatment for shock. When taken to City Hospital (see police report) was in state of collapse. Reached hospital 5:10 p.m., June 16th.
    The body is that of a thin but sufficiently nourished female. From condition of hands believe worked at domestic service, office cleaning,

or similar occupation. Clothing revealed nothing. There was no sign of violence on body.

There was no suicide note to be found. That the deceased was not anticipating death is possible, as a small paper bag containing darning silk was found in her purse. Also the report of the maid in said rest room, who states that the deceased was conscious when found, and said that she had been poisoned.

In view of the circumstances I am of the opinion that the cause of death was:

Administration of arsenical poison by person or persons unknown: Homicide.

(Signed) S. J. Wardwell
Chief Medical Examiner

AUTOPSY

Approximate age: *40 years*
Approximate weight: *115 lbs.*
Height: *5'3"*
Stenographer: John T. Heron

I hereby certify that on the 17th day of June, 1941, I, Richard M. Weaver, made an autopsy on this body eight hours after death, and said autopsy revealed:

No injury on body, which is that of a white female, apparently 40 years of age. Examination of viscera revealed characteristic symptoms of arsenical poisoning. Due to use of stomach pump impossible to tell time of last food taken. Possibly twelve hours before death.

Arsenic present in considerable amount in viscera.

(Signed) Richard M. Weaver
Assistant Medical Examiner

It was noon of the day after Ida disappeared before she was found at the morgue. The autopsy was over by that time, and Ida's tired hands were resting peacefully on a cold slab in the morgue when Carlton was taken there to identify her.

He gave one look and backed away.

"It's Ida, all right," he said hoarsely. "For God's sake, inspector! What's happening to us?"

"I imagine Ida knew too much," said the inspector, motioning the morgue master to push the body out of sight. "It's a pity. It's a cruel death."

He eyed Carlton thoughtfully.

"I've seen the reports," he said. "She went out yesterday without eating her lunch. At three o'clock or somewhat later she bought some darning silk at the notion counter of Stern and Jones. The saleswoman says she looked sick, and complained of cramps. The girl advised her to go to the rest room. She did. She sat in a chair at first. Then the maid got her to a couch, and called the store doctor. He says she didn't give her name or address, and by the time she got to the hospital she wasn't able to. It looks as though some time between the time she left the house and when she was found in the rest room she got the poison."

With Carlton looking on, he examined the clothing Ida had worn when taken to the hospital. It revealed nothing. Her bag, however, provided a shock. It contained no lipstick or powder. The coin purse had only a dollar or two. But tucked in a pocket behind a mirror were five new one-hundred-dollar bills.

The two men stared at them incredulously.

"You don't pay her in money like that?"

"Good heavens, no. Where did she get it?"

The notes were in series, and the inspector made a record

of their numbers. Then he sealed them in an envelope and ordered them put in the safe. Carlton was still unnerved when they reached the street. He lit a cigarette with shaking hands. But he was still fighting. He drew a long breath.

"At least this murder lets us out," he said. "None of us would kill the girl. And as for that money—"

"I suppose you were all at home yesterday afternoon after the inquest?"

Carlton flushed.

"You were there. You saw us. Except my sister. She was out shopping. But she would have no reason— You can't suspect *her* of this. She—"

The inspector cut in on him.

"Where does she usually shop?"

"At— I don't know. All over town, I imagine. What difference does it make? She was in Atlantic City when Mother died. And she was fond of Ida. You can't go on like this," he said, raising his voice. "You can't suspect all of us. It's damnable. It's crazy."

"We have had two murders," said the inspector stolidly. "There's a restaurant in Stern and Jones, isn't there?"

"I don't know. Marian ate her lunch after she left."

They parted there, Carlton stiffly to hail a taxi and go home, the inspector to go back to his office and call up certain banks. He found the one Carlton Fairbanks used, and asked them to check his account. After a brief wait he got the figures.

"Balance is three hundred and forty dollars. He drew out seventy-five in cash last week. That's all. Not suspecting him, are you, inspector?"

"No record of a withdrawal of five hundred in one-hundred-dollar bills in the last month or so?"

"No. He never has much of a balance."

It was one o'clock when he reached the Fairbanks house again. He interviewed the servants first. They were subdued and frightened. Even Amos had lost some of his surliness, and when they learned that Ida had been poisoned with arsenic there was a stricken silence. But they had nothing to tell him. Ida had taken Mrs. Fairbanks's death hard. She had eaten nothing in the house the day before after her breakfast, "and little enough of that." Asked where she kept her savings they agreed that she had an account at a downtown bank.

None of them believed for a moment that she had committed suicide.

"Why would she?" said Maggie practically. "She had a steady job and good pay. She wasn't the sort anyhow. She sent money every month to her people in the country. This will just about finish them," she added. "They're old, and farms don't pay any more. I suppose they've been notified?"

"Not yet. I want their address."

He took it down and asked for Hilda. William said she was in her room, and led him upstairs. She was sitting in a chair with her knitting in her lap, and he went in and closed the door behind him.

"I suppose you know?"

"Yes. There's a family conclave going on now in Marian's room."

"Overhear any of it?"

"I didn't try," she told him primly.

They went up the back stairs to Ida's room. Save for the preparations for lunch going on below the house was quiet, and Ida's room was as Hilda had seen it the day before. He searched it, but he found nothing of any importance. When he had finished Hilda handed him the piece of paper she had discovered.

"'Sorry,'" he read, "and 'harmless.' Part of a letter, isn't it? What do you suppose was harmless?"

"I think," said Hilda mildly, "that it was a snake. You see, the bats and the other things hadn't worked, so she tried a snake."

"Who tried a snake?"

"Ida."

"What on earth are you talking about? If you can make a snake out of the word 'harmless'—"

Hilda smiled.

"I didn't. I found one in my closet last night."

He was startled.

"Good God! How do you know it was harmless?"

"Well, there was that piece of paper, of course. And I saw it myself. Just a small garden snake. I wanted to take it out to the yard, but Carlton Fairbanks killed it. With a golf club," she added.

He inspected her, standing there in her neat white uniform, her face sweet and tranquil, and he felt a terrific desire to shake her.

"So it's as simple as that," he said caustically. "Ida puts it in your closet and Carlton kills it with a golf club." His voice rose. "What the hell has a snake got to do with two murders? And stop grinning at me."

"I'm not grinning," said Hilda with dignity. "I don't think Ida put it in the closet. I think it escaped from that hole in the wall, and it nearly scared Susie to death. But I do think Ida brought it here; it and the other things."

"Why?"

"Well, she was a country girl. She lived only thirty miles out of town, and she went there once a month or so. I was wondering," she added, "if I could go there this afternoon. They may know of her death, but they are old. It will be hard on them."

He gave her a suspicious look.

"That's all, is it? You wouldn't by any chance have something else in your mind?"

"It wouldn't hurt to look about a little," she said cautiously. "I think Doctor Brooke would drive me out."

He went to the window and stood looking out.

"Why would she do it?" he asked. "She had little or nothing to gain by the will."

"Oh, I don't think she killed Mrs. Fairbanks," Hilda said quickly. "She hated the house. The work was too heavy, for one thing. She may have wanted to scare her into moving."

"But you don't believe that?"

"I don't believe she killed herself. No."

Before he left he saw Carlton.

"In view of what has happened," he said, "I'd like to keep Miss Adams here for a day or two longer. You need not pay her. I'll attend to that."

"So we're to have a spy in the house," Carlton said bitterly. "What can I do about it? Let her stay, and the hell with it."

22.

Old Eliza Fairbanks was buried that afternoon from St. Luke's, with a cordon of police to hold back the crowd and photographers, holding cameras high, struggling for pictures of the family. Her small body in its heavy casket was carried into the church, and in due time out again. A long procession of cars drove up, filled, and drove away.

"What is it, a wedding?"

"Sh! It's a funeral. You know, the old woman who got stabbed."

Marian came out, her face bleak under her mourning. Carlton and Susie, Susie unashamedly crying. Jan, wan and lovely, but keeping her head high, and Courtney Brooke holding her arm. Nobody noticed Frank Garrison. He sat at the rear of the church, thinking God knows what; of his wedding perhaps in this same church, with Marian beside him; of Jan's christening at the font, a small, warm body in his arms; of Sunday mornings when he sat in the Fairbanks pew, and a little old lady sat beside him.

He got out quickly when it was over.

It was five o'clock when the family returned from the cemetery, and six before Hilda had got Marian to bed and was free. She went quietly out the side door and past the stable to Huston Street, to find Courtney waiting for her in his car.

"I hope we make it," he said. "The old bus does all right in town. When it stops I can have somebody fix it. But a trip like this—"

Hilda got in and settled herself.

"We'll make it," she said comfortably. "We've got to make it."

Yet at first there seemed nothing to discover. Two elderly people, stricken with grief, Ida's parents were only bewildered.

"Who would want to do that to her?" they asked.

"She was a good girl. She minded her own business. And she was fond of the family, miss. Especially Mrs. Garrison, Mrs. Marian Garrison. That's her picture there." Hilda looked. On the mantel was a photograph of Marian taken some years ago. "She was pretty then," the mother said. "Ida used to help her dress. She—"

She checked herself abruptly, and Hilda thought the father had made a gesture. She got nothing further from them. They knew nothing of any bats or other creatures, and Hilda, watching their surprise, was sure that it was genuine. They sat in the old-fashioned parlor, with an organ in the corner and a fan of paper in the empty fireplace, and denied that Ida had ever carried anything of the sort into town. "Why would she?"

"Some laboratories buy such things," Hilda said mendaciously, and got up. "Someone had been keeping things in a birdcage in the Fairbanks stable. Never mind. I'm only sorry. If there is anything I can do—"

Courtney had not gone into the house. He was standing by the car when she came out.

"Funny thing," he said. "There was a boy over by the barn. I started over to him but he beat it. Well, how did they take it?"

"It's broken them," she said wearily. "I suppose it was the boy who did it."

"Did what?"

"Caught the bats and so on and gave them to Ida."

He almost put the car into a ditch.

"So that's it," he said. "It was Ida! But why, and who killed her?"

"Are you sure you don't know, doctor? On the night Mrs. Fairbanks died you saw someone on the third floor, didn't you? You were holding a cup of coffee. It spilled."

He passed a truck before he replied.

"That's as preposterous a deduction as I've ever heard," he said. "If that's the way the police work—"

"I'm not a policewoman," she told him patiently. "You saw someone, didn't you?"

"I've already said no."

He was lying, and he was not a good liar. She did not pursue the subject. She was very quiet the rest of the way back to town. Her face had no longer its bland cherubic expression. She looked dispirited and half sick. When young Brooke politely but coldly offered her dinner at a roadhouse she refused it.

"I'm not hungry," she said. "Thanks just the same. I want to get back as soon as possible."

Yet for a woman in a hurry she did nothing much when she reached the Fairbanks house again. She did not get into uniform. She merely took off her hat and sat down in her room. When Jan, on her way to bed, rapped at her door she was still there in the dark.

"Good gracious! "Jan said. "Don't you want a light? And did you have anything to eat?"

"I didn't want anything, Jan."

"Just what were you and Courtney cooking up this afternoon?" Jan asked curiously. "I saw you, you know. You were gone for hours."

"I was telling Ida's people about her," said Hilda. "It was rather sad. I hate to carry bad news."

She looked at the girl. How would she bear another blow? Suppose she was right and Ida had been put out of the way because she knew what Hilda thought she knew?

It was midnight before she made any move. The household was asleep. Even Amos's light in the stable was out, by that time. But she took the precaution of slipping off her shoes. Then, armed with her flashlight, she went up to the third floor. She did not go back to Ida's room, however. She went into the guest rooms, taking one after the other, examining the floors and the bathrooms, and removing the dust covers from the beds.

It was in the room over Carlton's that she found what she had been afraid to find.

She went to bed and to sleep after that, but she carried a sort of mental alarm clock in her head, and promptly at six she wakened. Nobody was stirring in the house when she went down to the library and called the inspector on the phone at his bachelor apartment. His voice was heavy with sleep when he answered.

"It's Hilda Adams," she said carefully. "I want you to do something. Now, if you will."

"At this hour? Good heavens, Hilda, don't you ever go to bed?"

"I do, but I get out of it. Will you have someone check the

hotels in town for a woman who got there early Sunday morning and left that afternoon?"

"Sunday? Sure. But what's it all about?"

"I'll tell you later. I can't talk here."

She hung up and went upstairs again. She had been stupid, she thought. She should have known all this before. Yet she had also a sense of horror. It was still written all over her when she sat in the inspector's office that Wednesday morning.

"How did you guess it?" he said.

"Then it's correct?"

"Correct as hell. She checked in at five Sunday morning and left that afternoon. She left Atlantic City on Saturday."

She drew a long breath.

"I should have known it before," she said. "The figure at the top of the stairs and the chandelier shaking. I think young Brooke saw it, too, although he denies it. But the rooms looked the same. Only Ida had cleaned a bathroom, and she couldn't put back the dust. I suppose that cost her her life. If she had only raised a window and let the dirt in—"

In spite of himself Fuller smiled.

"The world lost a great criminal in you, Hilda," he said admiringly.

He looked over his notes. Marian had registered at one of the big Atlantic City hotels the night she had left home. She had remained most of the time in her room, having her meals served there, and she had left on a late train on Saturday.

"It checks," he said thoughtfully. "She came home late and Ida probably admitted her and told her Eileen was there. She smuggled her up the back stairs to the third floor and settled her there. Then what? Did she come down while young Brooke was with Jan, and stab her mother? It's—well, it's unnatural, to say the least."

Hilda sat very still.

"I'm not sure," she said at last. "She was there. I don't know where she hid while the house was searched. Maybe in the stable. Anyhow she got away, and after you let Ida go I suppose she made up the bed."

"What put you on the track?" he asked curiously.

"I don't know exactly." She got up to go. "Ida's parents said she was devoted to Marian. And then the doctor—I just wondered if Ida had seen Marian at Stern and Jones on Monday."

He looked at her with shocked surprise.

"You don't mean that, do you?"

"It could be," she said rather dismally, and went out.

He read over his notes carefully after she had gone. The waitresses in the restaurant at Stern & Jones did not remember Ida, but they did remember Marian, who was well known in the store. She had come in at three o'clock and had a cup of tea. But she had been alone. As to the will, in a long-distance call to Mrs. Fairbanks's lawyer, Charles Willis, in Canada for salmon, Willis said that the old lady had kept all three copies, but that Carlton was substantially correct. The estate was divided between Marian and Carlton, with Marian's share in trust for Janice.

"Although there was a hundred thousand dollars for the girl," he said.

The will had been made seven years ago. He did not think she had changed it.

After that the inspector went to Mrs. Fairbanks's bank, and had some difficulty in getting information. In the end, however, he learned that over the past year or two she had been selling bonds and converting the results into cash. This she apparently deposited in the safe-deposit boxes in the basement, of which she rented several. If she had removed this cash the bank had no knowledge of it. It was not an unusual procedure, especially where the customer was a woman. Women resented both income and inheritance taxes, always hoping to escape them. And here the bank added a human note. "As do most people," it said.

Back at his office he made a brief chronological chart:

In January, Susie had seen Mrs. Fairbanks remove cash from the bank and take it to her box.

In February, Mrs. Fairbanks and Marian had gone to Florida, while the safe was installed, and Susie's brother-in-law built the peephole.

On the ninth of March Mrs. Fairbanks came home, arriving that night. The next morning she was poisoned with arsenic. The arsenic was shown to have been in the sugar.

She was suspicious afterward of her household, making her own breakfast and at other meals eating only what they ate. But the attempt had not been repeated. From that day in March until the beginning of May everything had been as usual.

After that the so-called hauntings began. It was the first of May when she found the first bat in her room. Later there were two more bats, two sparrows, and a rat over a period of a month, and when another bat was discovered she had gone to the police.

"Someone is trying to kill me," she had said, sitting erect in her chair. "I have a bad heart, and they know it. But I'm pretty hard to scare."

He put his notes away and went thoughtfully out to lunch.

He saw Courtney Brooke that afternoon, and he laid all his

cards on the table. He liked the boy, but he sensed a change in him when it came to the safe and the money possibly in it. He stiffened slightly.

"I don't care a damn for the money," he said. "As a matter of fact it bothers me. I'd rather marry a poor girl. I suppose you can open the safe, sooner or later?"

"It won't be easy. The makers will send somebody, if we don't find the combination. I'm putting a guard in the grounds to-night. If the money is there, it won't leave the house."

But Brooke still looked uneasy, and Fuller changed the subject. He asked about arsenic. It could be obtained without much trouble, the doctor said; weed killers, of course, but also it could be soaked out of fly-paper, for instance, or even out of old wallpapers and some fabrics. But on the subject of the attack on Jan he waxed bitter.

"Who would want to kill her? The old lady and Ida, well, the old lady had the money and Ida probably knew something. But to try to kill Jan—"

"I don't think anyone tried to kill her."

Brooke stared.

"Look at it," said the inspector. "She could have been killed. She was unconscious, and the nurse was locked up in Amos's rooms. But she wasn't killed. She probably began to come to, and she was struck to put her out again. Somebody was there who didn't want to be seen."

Brooke said nothing. He gazed out the window, looking thoughtful, as though he was comparing all this with some private knowledge of his own. When he turned to the inspector it was with a faint smile.

"Funny," he said. "I've been scared to hell and gone. You've relieved me a lot. I've been hanging around under the window every night since it happened."

But the smile died when he was asked about the night of Mrs. Fairbanks's death.

"I didn't see anybody on the third floor," he said flatly. "That's Miss Adams's idea. Just because I spilled some coffee—"

"I think you did," said the inspector, his face grave. "I think you saw Marian Fairbanks, and she saw you."

"How could I? She wasn't there."

"Just whom did you see, doctor?"

"Nobody," he asserted stubbornly. "Nobody at all."

23.

IDA HAD been poisoned on Monday, and Mrs. Fairbanks was buried on Tuesday. It was Wednesday morning when Hilda made her report, and it was the same night when Frank Garrison was arrested for murder.

Late on Wednesday afternoon Fuller went back to the Fairbanks house. He intended interviewing Marian, and he dreaded doing it. To believe that she had killed her mother and a servant and attacked her own child made her an inhuman monster. Unhappy and bitter as she was, he did not believe she was guilty. Nor, he thought, did Hilda.

He did not interview her, however. Marian was in bed, under the influence of a sedative, and he found Hilda back in uniform at her old post in the hall. An absorbed Hilda, who was not knitting or reading the Practice of Nursing, but instead had set up a card table and was patiently laying out a pack of cards.

"And people pay you money for this!" he said. "I wish my job was as easy."

She nodded absently, and he watched her as she gathered up the cards, closely inspected the edges, and then began to lay them out again. He sat down and watched her.

"What is all this?"

"I'll tell you in a minute." She was intensely serious. "It's the order," she said. "Clubs first don't do. Maybe it's the other way. Spades."

"Nothing has disturbed you, has it? You feel all right? No dizzy spells? Anything like that?"

She did not even hear him. She spread the cards again, gathered them up, looked at the edges, spread them slightly, and then handed him the pack.

There was something written on one side, and she looked rather smug.

"I think it's the combination to the safe," she said complacently.

Fuller examined the cards. Thus arranged they showed plainly written in ink a series of letters and numbers. Shuffled in the ordinary fashion they were not detectable, but in their present order they were perfectly clear. He gave her an odd look. Then he took out an old envelope and wrote them down.

"So that's the solitaire she played," he said thoughtfully. "Good girl, Hilda. How did you think of it?"

"Courtney Brooke thought of it first," she told him.

He eyed her sharply, but her face told him nothing.

He sent for Carlton before they opened the safe. He had little or nothing to say. He did not even ask how they had found the combination. Hilda unlocked the door, and he followed them in. The room was as it had been left after the search, and he carefully avoided looking at it. There was still daylight, but the closet was dark and Hilda brought a flashlight. Using it the inspector turned the dial, but he did not open the door.

"I'd rather you did this, Fairbanks," he said.

He stepped out of the closet, and Carlton stepped in. He

pulled open the door and looked speechlessly inside. The safe was packed to the top with bundles of currency.

He made a little gesture and backed out of the closet. He looked small and singularly defenseless.

"All right. It's there," he said dully. "Do what you like with it. I don't want to look at it. It makes me sick."

It required some urging to send him back again.

"Look for your mother's will," Fuller said. "Bring out any papers you find. We may learn something."

The will was there, in a compartment of its own. It was in a brown envelope sealed with red wax, and it was marked *Last Will and Testament* in the old lady's thin hand. Carlton almost broke down when he read it. But there was another paper in the envelope, and he opened and read it, too. He stood, against the absurd background of hanging fussy dresses and shoes in the bag on the door, holding the paper and staring at it. But neither Hilda nor the inspector was prepared for his reaction to it.

"So that's why she was killed," he said thickly, and collapsed on the floor before they could reach him.

Frank Garrison was arrested late that night at his club. He was evidently living there. His clothes were in the closet, his brushes on the dresser, and he was in pajamas when they found him.

He said little or nothing. The inspector had sent the detectives out, and remained himself in the room while he dressed. Once he said he better take his bag "as he might not be coming back soon." And again he spoke of Jan.

"Tell the poor kid to take it easy, will you?" he said. "She's had enough trouble, and she's—fond of me."

He puzzled the inspector. He offered no explanation of his

being at the club. He offered nothing, in fact. He sat in the car, his fine profile etched against the street lights, and except once when he lit a cigarette he did not move. He seemed to be thinking profoundly. Nor was he more co-operative when they reached the inspector's office, with two or three detectives around, and a stenographer taking down questions and answers.

He was perfectly polite. He denied absolutely having been in the Fairbanks house the night Mrs. Fairbanks was killed, although he admitted having been in the grounds.

"I came home late from Washington. The apartment was empty—we had not had a maid for some time—and my wife was not there. I knew Jan was friendly with Eileen, so I went there to ask if she knew what had happened. We had quarreled, and I was afraid she—well, she's been pretty nervous lately. But Jan—my daughter—said she was there. I talked to Jan at her window. I did not enter the house."

"What did you do after that?"

"I walked around for a while. Then I went home."

"What time did you talk to your daughter?"

"After one. Perhaps half past. I didn't get back from Washington until twelve o'clock."

"Did your daughter tell you where your wife was? In what room?"

He colored.

"Yes. In my former wife's bedroom. I didn't like it, but what could I do?"

"She told you your wife was sick?"

"Yes."

"You didn't come in, to see how she was?"

"We had quarreled before I left. I didn't think she cared to see me. Anyhow, her light was out. I thought she was asleep."

"You have since separated?"

"Not exactly. Call it a difference."

"She is going to have a child."

He showed temper for the first time.

"What the hell has that got to do with this?"

But although he was guardedly frank about his movements the night of Mrs. Fairbanks's murder, he continued to deny having entered the house, through Eileen's window or in any other way. He had not climbed to the roof of the porte-cochere. He doubted if it was possible. And when he was shown the knife he stated flatly that he had never to his knowledge seen it before. He admitted, however, knowing that the safe was in Mrs. Fairbanks's room. "Jan told me about it." But he denied any knowledge whatever of its contents.

The mention of the safe, however, obviously disturbed him. He seemed relieved when the subject was changed to the attack on Jan in the loft of the stable; but he was clearly indignant about it, as well as puzzled.

"If I could lay my hands on whoever did it I—well, I might commit a murder of my own."

"You have no explanation of it?"

They thought he hesitated.

"None whatever. Unless she was mistaken for someone else. Or—" he added slowly—"unless someone was there who didn't want to be seen."

They shifted to Ida's death. He seemed puzzled.

"You knew her?"

"Of course. She had been in the Fairbanks house for years."

"She was attached to your first wife?"

"I don't know. I don't care to discuss my first wife."

"You are on good terms?"

"Good God, leave her out of this, can't you? I won't have her dragged in. What has she got to do with it, or my—feeling for her?"

He was excited, indignant. The inspector broke the tension.

"Mr. Garrison, did you at any time in the last few weeks supply this woman, Ida Miller, with certain creatures to introduce into Mrs. Fairbanks's room?" He picked up a memorandum and read from it. "'Five bats, two sparrows, one or more rats, and a small garden snake.'"

The detective grinned. The stenographer dropped his pen. And Frank Garrison unexpectedly laughed. Only the inspector remained sober.

"Is that a serious question?"

"It is."

"The answer is no. I thought the old lady imagined all that."

"Have you at any time had in your possession a poison called arsenious acid? White arsenic?"

"Never."

"Can you account for your movements Monday afternoon? Say, from one o'clock on."

The quick shifts seemed to bother him, but he managed to make a fair statement. He had lunched at the club. After that he went to see a man who was taking over some housing work in Washington. When he went home his wife was still in bed. She had been "difficult." He had told her he would send her a maid. After that he had packed a bag and left. They had not been getting on for some time. Perhaps it was his fault. He wasn't accustomed to being idle.

"Did you at any time Monday go to Stern and Jones? The department store?"

"I stopped in and bought a black tie. I was going to Mrs. Fairbanks's funeral the next day."

"At what time?"

"After I saw the man I referred to. Maybe two-thirty or three o'clock."

"Did you see the girl, Ida, at that time?"

He looked puzzled.

"Where? Where would I see her?"

"In the store."

"No. Certainly not."

"Have you a key to the Fairbanks house?"

"I may have, somewhere. I lived there for a good many years. I don't carry it."

It lasted until half past one. The questions were designed to confuse him, but on the whole he kept his head. It was not until the inspector lifted a paper from the desk and handed it to him that he apparently gave up the fight. He glanced at it and handed it back, his face set.

"I see," he said quietly. "I was there that night. I could have got into the house, by key or through my wife's window, and I had a motive. I suppose that's enough."

"You knew about this agreement?"

"Mrs. Fairbanks told me about it at the time."

"Who else knew about it?"

"My first wife. She signed it, as you see. Mrs. Fairbanks and myself."

"No one else knew about it?"

"Not unless Mrs. Fairbanks told about it. I don't think she did."

The inspector got up. He looked tired, and for once uncertain.

"I'm sorry about this, Garrison," he said. "We're not through, but I'll have to hold you. We'll see that you're not too uncomfortable."

Garrison forced a smile and stood.

"No rubber hose?" he said.

"No rubber hose," said the inspector.

There was a momentary silence. Garrison glanced around the room. He seemed on the point of saying something, something important. The hush was breathless, as if all the men were waiting and watching. But he decided against it, whatever it was.

"I suppose it's no use saying I didn't do it?"

"No man is guilty until he has been found guilty," said the inspector sententiously, and watched the prisoner out of the room.

Carlton broke the news to the family the next morning, a worried little man, telling Susie first, staying with Jan until she had stopped crying, and then going to Marian. He was there a long time. Hilda, shut out, could hear his voice and Marian's loud hysterical protests.

"He never did it. Never. Never."

When the inspector came she refused at first to see him, and he went in to find her sitting frozen in a chair and gazing ahead of her as though she was seeing something she did not want to face. She turned her head, however, at his crisp greeting.

"Good morning," he said. "Do you mind if we have a little talk?"

"I have no option, have I?"

"I can't force you, you know," he said matter-of-factly. "All I would like is a little co-operation."

"Co-operation!" she said, her face set and cold. "Why should I co-operate? You are holding Frank Garrison, aren't you? Of all the cruel absurd things! A man who loved my mother! The kindest man on earth! What possible reason could he have had to kill my mother?"

"There was a possible reason, and you know it, Mrs. Garrison," he said unsmilingly.

He drew up a chair and sat down, confronting her squarely.

"At what time did you reach here, the night your mother was killed?" he asked.

It was apparently the one question she had not expected. She opened her mouth to speak, but she could not. She tried to get out of her chair, and the inspector put his hand on her knee.

"Better sit still," he said quietly. "You had every right to be here. I am not accusing you of anything. Suppose I help you a little. You came home during or after the time your husband's present wife had arrived. Either you saw her, in the hall downstairs, or one of the servants told you she was here. However that was, you decided to stay. It was your house. Why let her drive you out? Is that right?"

"Yes," she said, with tight lips. "It was Ida. I opened the side door with my latchkey. There was no one around, so I went back to get William to carry up my bags. I met Ida in the back hall. She told me."

She went on. She seemed glad to talk. She had been angry and indignant. She didn't even want to see Jan. It was Jan who had brought it about. Jan had said that Eileen was going to have a baby, and had even brought her to the house. That was why she had gone away. To have her own mother and her own child against her! And now Eileen had invented some silly story and sought sanctuary here.

"I wasn't going to let her drive me away a second time," she said. "She had ruined my life, and now at my mother's orders they had put her in my room. I couldn't believe it at first, when Ida told me."

Ida, it appeared, had got her to the third floor by the back staircase, and made up the bed. They had to walk carefully, for fear Carlton would hear them in his room below. But she did not go to bed. How could she, with that woman below? She did manage to smoke, sitting by the open window. She was still sitting there when Susie began to scream.

"That was when Ida came to warn you?"

"She knew something was terribly wrong. Neither of us knew what. I thought at first the house was on fire. I sent her down, and listened over the stair rail. That's how I knew what had happened."

She sat back. Her color was better now, and the inspector, watching her, thought she looked like a woman who had passed a danger point safely.

"No one but Ida knew you were in the house?" he persisted.

"No one. Not even Jan."

"Are you sure of that? Didn't you come down the stairs while Doctor Brooke was in the hall?"

"Never."

But she looked shaken. Her thin hands were trembling.

"I think you did, Mrs. Garrison," he told her. "He was standing outside your mother's door. You spoke to him from the stairs.

You told him to get Eileen out of the house in the morning, didn't you?"

"No! I did nothing of the sort," said Marian frantically. There was complete despair in her face. She looked beaten. "I never spoke to him at all," she said in a dead voice. "When I saw him he was coming out of Mother's room."

The rest of her story was not important. She told it with dead eyes and in a flat hopeless voice. Brooke had not seen her, she thought, and Ida had helped her to get out of the house before the police had taken charge. She had used the back stairs and had gone out through the break in the fence. She had taken only the one bag which she could carry, Ida hiding the other, and she had spent what was left of the night at a hotel.

"I was afraid to stay," she told them. "After what I'd seen I didn't want to be questioned. I had Jan to think of. I still have Jan to think of," she added drearily. "Courtney Brooke killed my mother, and I've ruined Jan's life forever and ever."

24.

BROOKE WAS interrogated at police headquarters that afternoon. Inspector Fuller found him in his back office, dressing a small boy's hand.

"All right, Jimmy," he said. "And don't fool with knives after this."

The boy left, and Fuller went in. Young Brooke was putting away his dressings, his face sober.

"What's this about Mr. Garrison being held, inspector?" he said. "I was just going over to see Jan. She's taking it badly."

The inspector did not relax.

"You've been holding out on us, doctor," he said stiffly. "That's a dangerous thing to do in a murder case."

Brooke flushed. He still held a roll of bandage in his hand. He put it down on the table before he answered.

"All right. What's it all about?"

"You were in Mrs. Fairbanks's room at or about the time she was killed."

"Why not?" He looked defiant. "She was my patient. I had a right to look at her. She'd had a good bit of excitement that night, and I didn't go all the way in. I opened the door and listened. She was alive then. I'll swear to that. I could hear her breathing."

"Why didn't you tell about it?" said the inspector inexorably.

Brooke looked unhappy.

"Sheer funk, I suppose. I told Jan, after it all came out, and she didn't want me to. Not that I'm putting the blame on her," he added quickly. "I was in a cold sweat myself. In fact, I still am!"

He grinned and pulling out a handkerchief mopped his face.

"I thought I had as many guts as the other fellow," he said. "But this thing's got me."

He looked incredulous, however, when the inspector asked him to go with him to headquarters.

"What for? Are you trying to arrest me?" he asked suspiciously.

"Not necessarily. We'll want a statement from you."

"I've told you everything I know."

He went finally, calling to the slovenly girl that he would be back for dinner, and slamming the door furiously behind him as he left the house. He was still indignant when he reached the inspector's office. A look at the room, however, with the stenographer at his desk and Captain Henderson and the detectives filing in, rather subdued him.

"Third-degree stuff, I suppose," he said, and lit a cigarette. "All right. I'm a fool and a coward, but I'm no killer. You can put that down."

"No third degree, doctor. Just some facts. Sit down, please. We may be some time."

They were some time. Before they were through he was white and exhausted.

"Did Janice Garrison know of the document in the safe?"

"Yes. Why drag her in? She hasn't done anything."

"She was fond of her father?"

"Crazy about him."

"You knew that she was to inherit a considerable sum of money?"

"I did."

"What were your exact movements, the night Mrs. Fairbanks was killed? While the nurse was downstairs boiling water?"

"I cleaned the hypo with alcohol. After that I looked in at Mrs. Fairbanks. She was breathing all right, so I went back to see Jan. I was there about five minutes. I went back and poured some coffee. I was drinking it when the nurse came up with the water."

"At what time did you see Mrs. Garrison?"

He was startled.

"Mrs. Garrison! She wasn't there. She didn't come until the next day. Sunday."

"She was there, doctor. She saw you coming out of her mother's room."

"Oh, God," he said wretchedly. "So she was there, too. Poor Jan!"

But his story was straightforward. He had not seen Marian when he came out of Mrs. Fairbanks's room. Later, however, as he poured the coffee, he had felt that someone was overhead, on the third floor. The glass chandelier was shaking. He had looked up the staircase, but no one was in sight.

They showed him the knife, and he smiled thinly.

"Never saw it before," he said. He examined it. "Somebody did a rotten job of sharpening it," he said.

"It seems to have answered," the inspector observed dryly. "Have you ever done any surgery, doctor?"

"Plenty."

"You could find a heart without trouble? Even in the dark?"

"Anybody can find a heart. It's bigger than most people think. But if you mean did I stab Mrs. Fairbanks, certainly not."

He explained readily enough his search and Jan's for the combination of the safe.

"She knew the agreement was there. The old lady had told her. She was afraid it would incriminate her father. When nobody could open the safe I happened to think of the cards. Mrs. Fairbanks played solitaire at night. But maybe she didn't. Jan believed she locked herself in and then opened the safe, and we thought the cards might have the combination. I'd seen them with pictures painted on the edges. You arranged them a certain way and there was the picture."

"The idea being to get this document?"

"Well, yes. She was worrying herself sick. But the nurse was too smart for us. She locked the door."

It was five o'clock before he was released, with a warning not to leave town. He managed to grin at that. He got out his wallet and some silver from his pocket.

"I could travel—let's see—exactly five dollars and eighty cents' worth," he said. "I've just paid the rent."

The inspector looked at Henderson after he had gone.

"Well?" he said.

"Could have," said Henderson. "But my money's on the other fellow. Garrison was broke, too, but he wouldn't be without the alimony."

"Why didn't he have it reduced? It would have been easier than murder."

"Still in love with the first wife," said Henderson promptly. "Sticks out all over him."

"Oh," said the inspector. "So you got that, too!"

Alone in his office he got out the document he had shown to Garrison the night before, and studied it. Briefly it was an agreement written in the old lady's hand, signed by Marian and witnessed by Amos and Ida, by which Marian's alimony from her ex-husband was to cease on her mother's death. "Otherwise, as provided for in my will, she ceases to inherit any portion of my estate save the sum of one dollar, to be paid by my executors."

He had a picture of Mrs. Fairbanks writing that, all the resentment at Marian and the divorce and its terms in her small resolute body and trembling old hand. He put it back in his safe, along with the knife and Hilda's contributions—a can of white paint, a pair of worn chauffeur's driving gloves, a bit of charred rope, a largish square of unbleached muslin, and now a pack of playing cards. To that odd assortment he added the paper on which he had recorded the numbers of the new bills in Ida's purse, and surveyed the lot glumly.

"Looks like Bundles for Britain," he grunted.

He saw Eileen late that afternoon. She was in bed, untidy and tearful, and she turned on him like a wildcat.

"I always knew the police were fools," she shrieked. "What have you got on Frank Garrison? Nothing, and you know it. I didn't let him in through my window. I didn't let anybody in. I was sick. Why don't you ask the doctor? He knows."

He could get nothing from her. She turned sulky and then cried hysterically. She didn't know about Mrs. Fairbanks's will.

She had never heard of any agreement. What sort of an agreement? And they'd better release Frank if they knew what was good for them. She'd get a lawyer. She'd get a dozen lawyers. She would take it to the President. She would take it to the Supreme Court. She would—

This new conception of the Supreme Court at least got him away. He left her still talking, and when the maid let him out he suggested a doctor.

"She's pretty nervous," he said. Which was by way of being a masterpiece of understatement.

On the way downtown he thought he saw Hilda in one of the shopping streets, but when he stopped his car and looked back she had disappeared.

He might have been surprised, had he followed her.

25.

HILDA WAS at a loose end that afternoon. Courtney had recovered from his collapse and had gone out, still pale, to drive around in his car and think his own unhappy thoughts. Marian's door had been closed and locked since the inspector's visit. Jan wandered around the house, worried about her mother and ignorant of what was going on. And Susie, recovered from her fright about her husband, had settled down on her bed to a magazine.

"I'd better loaf while I can," she told Hilda. "It's me for the pigpens from now on. If you think Carl will change his mind now that he gets some money you can think again."

Hilda was standing in the doorway, her face bland but her eyes alert.

"What do you think about the police holding Mr. Garrison?" she asked.

"Me? They're crazy. Carl says that paper they found will convict him, but I don't believe it. If you ask me—"

She stopped abruptly.

"If I asked you, what?"

"Nothing," said Susie airily. "If I were you I'd take a look at the radio by Mrs. Fairbanks's bed. Maybe you can make something out of it. I can't."

"What's wrong with it?"

"I don't know. It's set to a blank spot on the dial. That's all. Carl says he didn't move the needle."

She went back to her magazine, and Hilda went to the old lady's room. She closed the door and going to the radio switched it on. There was a faint roaring as the tubes warmed up, but nothing else. She was puzzled rather than excited. But she had already decided to go out, and now she had a double errand.

Her first errand was to the ladies' room of Stern & Jones. The attendant was the same woman who had looked after Ida, and she was immediately loquacious.

"A friend of hers, are you?" she said. "Wasn't it dreadful? And nobody knowing who she was all that time!"

"Was she very sick when she got here?"

"She looked terrible. I asked her if she had had anything that disagreed with her, and she said only a cup of tea. I called up the tearoom right away. Some of the girls had gone, but nobody remembered her. Anyhow, our tea is all right. It could not have been that, or a lot of other people would have been sick too."

"Is that all she said?"

"Well, she tried to tell me where she lived. She wanted to go home. Grove Avenue, I think she said. But after that she got so bad she couldn't talk at all."

Hilda was filled with cold anger when she left the store. The thought of Ida, dying and unable to tell who she was, enraged her. And now the radio assumed a new importance. If it had been turned to a blank spot on the dial and still played, the whole situation changed. Mrs. Fairbanks might have been already dead when it was turned on.

She visited a number of stores where radio sets were sold, including Stern & Jones. Some of them had remote controls. The boxes they showed her were only a foot long and four inches wide, and they operated as far as sixty feet from the instrument.

"You can set it out in the street," said one salesman, "and turn your radio on and off with it. Magic, ain't it?"

Sixty feet! That would include even Marian's room. But when she told the make and age of the machine the man shook his head.

"Sorry," he said. "It wouldn't work on one of those old ones. Not a chance."

It was the same everywhere. The machine in Mrs. Fairbanks's room was too old. And the remote controls which used cables were not only modern. They required considerable time for adjustment. But in the end she found something.

She was tired and her feet ached when at six o'clock she got back to the house, going directly to the kitchen. William was on the back porch, relaxing in the summer sun, and Maggie was baking a cake. She turned a red face from the oven when Hilda drew a chair to the kitchen table and sat down. But some of Maggie's suspicions had died in the last few days. She even offered her a cup of tea.

Hilda, however, was definitely off tea, at least for a time.

"I'd like a glass of water," she said. "Then I want to talk about Ida."

"I'm not talking about Ida," Maggie said stiffly.

"If anyone thinks she got that stuff here in this house—"

"I'm not asking about her death. That's for the police. It's just this. Have you any idea why she carried those blankets out to Amos?"

"No. He didn't need them."

"Can you remember what happened that day? It was the day after Mrs. Fairbanks was killed, wasn't it?"

Maggie considered this.

"You know how she was that morning. She was so bad I sent her up to rest. She came down later, and that was when Amos says she carried out the blankets. I didn't see her myself. All I know is she didn't eat any lunch. She left when we were sitting down."

Hilda drank her water and went out to the stable. To her annoyance Amos, in his shirt sleeves, was smoking a pipe inside the garage. He was reading the paper, his chair tilted back. He looked up when he saw her.

"Anything I can do for you, miss?"

He grinned with his usual slyness, and Hilda regarded him with disfavor.

"You can come up to the loft with me," she said coldly. "And don't smirk at me, I don't like it."

Thus reduced, Amos followed her up the stairs. There was still light enough to see around, and to her shocked surprise she found the entire place had been swept and put in order.

"Who did this?" she said sharply.

He grinned.

"I did," he said. "Anything to say about it, Miss Policewoman? Any reason why I can't clean the place I live in?"

She ignored that, looking around her carefully. She had had very little hope at any time, but she disliked giving up. Amos was grinning again, pleased at her discomfiture.

"That isn't funny," she said. "I want some answers, and if I don't get them the police will. When you cleaned this place did you find anything that didn't belong? That you hadn't seen here before?"

The mention of the police sobered him.

"Nothing new. Only the birdcage was on the floor. It used to be in the cupola, when Ida kept her bats and things in it. Wrapped it in a cloth, she did. I threw it out."

"Oh!" she said blankly. "You knew it was Ida, did you?"

"Well, when a woman gets an old birdcage and a net and keeps climbing at night into that tower up there, I didn't think she was after butterflies, and that's a fact."

"Did you tell anybody, Amos?"

"Not me," he said negligently. "Bats don't hurt anybody. Let her have her fun, said I. She didn't have much."

She looked at him. He was incredible, this stocky individualist who had believed in letting Ida have what he called her fun, and who apparently knew far more than he had even indicated. It amused him to tell her so, leaning against one of the trunks and now and then sucking at his dead pipe. Indeed, once started it was hard to stop him. He said that one night Carlton came and, getting the cage, carried it to the house. It was empty, as he—Amos—happened to know. But he had brought it back before morning. He said it was Frank Garrison who had caught Susie by the garage the night Mrs. Fairbanks was murdered. He'd seen him. And he observed cheerfully that he knew Marian had been in the house that same night.

"Funniest sight I most ever saw," he said, his shrewd eyes on hers. "Her streaking across the grass in her nightgown when the police cars were coming in. I slid down and unlocked the door, but she never saw me. She hid in the loft until Ida brought her clothes and bags. Toward morning, it was."

"Why didn't you tell it at the time, Amos?"

"Nobody asked me."

She felt helpless before the vast indifference, the monumental ego of the man. But she had not finished with him.

"Why did Ida have those creatures, Amos? Was it to scare Mrs. Fairbanks away? After all, she had worked here for years."

He grinned at her slyly.

"Maybe she didn't like her," he said. "Or maybe she didn't like the stairs. Lots of climbing in the house. May have wanted her to move to an apartment. I've heard her say as much."

"I suppose you know how she got them into the room, too?"

"Sure," he said, and grinned again. "Through Mrs. Carlton Fairbanks's peephole in the closet."

She left him then. She felt that even now he might have certain reserves, certain suspicions. But he did not intend to tell them. She could see that in his face.

"So they've arrested Mr. Garrison," he said as she went down the stairs. "Mr. Garrison and the doc across the street. Don't let them fool you, Miss Policewoman. They'll have to eat crow before they're through." He seemed to think this was humorous. He laughed. "But I'd like to know how Ida felt when she got that snake," he said. "I'll bet she didn't like it."

"So there is something you don't know!" said Hilda coldly, and went back to the house.

Nevertheless, she had a curious feeling about Amos as she left him. As though he had been trying to tell her something. As though he was hoping that she would see what he could not tell her. And there had been something in his small sly eyes which looked like grief; a deep and tragic grief.

When she went upstairs she found Jan in the upper hall.

"She's still sleeping," she said. "I suppose she needs it, Miss

Adams. They won't hold Father long, will they? They must know he didn't do it."

Evidently she did not know about Courtney, and Hilda said nothing. She tried the door to Marian's room and found it locked.

"How long has she been asleep, Jan?" she asked.

"I don't know. She's been in there since the inspector left. It's seven now."

Hilda rapped on the door. Then she pounded hard and called. There was no response, however. Jan was standing by, looking terrified.

"You don't think she's—"

"She's probably taken an overdose of sleeping medicine," Hilda said briskly. "Get a doctor. If you can't get Courtney Brooke get someone else. And hurry."

It was Brooke who came, running across the yard and reaching the house as Amos and William were lifting a ladder to the porte-cochere. He shoved them aside and climbed up. A moment later the screen gave way and he unlocked and opened the door into the hall.

"She's still breathing," he said. "Go away, Jan. I don't want you here. She'll be all right."

Hilda went in, and he closed the door behind her. Marian was lying on the bed, not moving. She looked peaceful and lovely, almost beautiful, as though that deep sleep of hers had erased the lines from her face and brought back some of her youth. But she was very far gone.

Brooke examined her and threw off his coat.

"Come on, Miss Adams," he said. "We've got to get busy if we're going to save her."

26.

At nine o'clock that same night a young man carrying a parcel arrived at the house and asked for Hilda. William brought the message to Marian's door.

"Tell him to wait," she said briefly. "Put him in the morning room and close the door. Tell him he's to stay if it takes all night."

William hesitated, his old head shaking.

"How is she, miss?"

"A little better."

"Thank God for that," he said and tottered down the stairs.

It was ten o'clock when Courtney Brooke went out into the hall and, bending over, kissed Jan gently.

"It's all right, darling. You can see her for a minute. Don't talk to her."

When Jan came out he was waiting. He took her back to her room and put his arms around her.

"My girl," he said. "Always and ever my girl, sweet. Hold on to me, darling. You need somebody to hold on to, don't you? And I'm strong. I'll never let you down."

"I've had so much, Court!"

"You've had too much, sweet. But it's all over. There won't be any more."

She looked up into his eyes, steady and honest, and drew a long breath.

"Why did she do it, Court? Was it because Father—"

"Your father's all right. Take my word for it, darling."

"Then who—"

"Hush," he said, cradling her in his arms. "Hush, my sweet. Don't think. Don't worry. It's all over. You're to rest now. Just rest." He picked her up and laid her gently on the bed. "Sleep if you can. Think of me if you can't! Look out, darling. There's a moon. I ordered it for tonight, for you."

She lay still, after he had gone, looking at the moon. She felt very tired, but she was peaceful, too. It was over. Court had said so. She wrapped herself in his promise like a blanket, and fell asleep. She was still asleep when, at eleven, the inspector drove in under the porte-cochere.

Susie and Carlton were in the library. Carlton's face was haggard, and even Susie looked stricken. She could accept murder, but she could not face suicide, or the attempt at it. Life was too important to her, the love of it too strong.

She sat beside Carl, his head drawn down on her shoulder, her eyes soft.

"Don't be a jackass," she said. "Of course she didn't do it."

"Then why would she try to kill herself?"

"Because she's the same kind of fool I am. Because she's a one-man woman." She sat up and lit a cigarette. "Let's forget it," she said. "Let's think about a farm. You can raise what you want, and I'll raise pigs. I rather like pigs," she said. "At least they're natural. They don't pretend to be anything but pigs."

"So long as you're around, old girl," he said huskily. "So long as you're around."

They did not hear the inspector as he went up the stairs and tiptoed into Mrs. Fairbanks's room, closing the door behind him. He did not turn on a light, or sit down. Instead, he went to a window and stood looking out. The whole thing was not to his taste. He had come at Hilda's request, and it was not like her to be dramatic. So Marian Garrison had tried to kill herself! It might be a confession, or the equivalent of one. And where the hell was Hilda, anyhow?

He was rapidly becoming indignant when suddenly without warning the radio behind him roared into action. He almost leaped into the air with the shock. It was playing the Habanera from *Carmen*, and the din was terrific. He was turning on the lights when Hilda came in.

For the first time in his experience she looked frightened. She shut off the machine and confronted him.

"That's how it was done," she said, and sat down weakly in a chair.

"What do you mean, that's how?"

She did not answer directly. She looked tired and unhappy.

"It's a phonograph. You set the radio dial on to a certain place and turn it on. It's a blank spot, where there's no station. Nothing happens, of course. But if you've got this machine plugged in on the same circuit, even in another room, it plays through the radio. As it did here."

"There was no phonograph in the house that night," he said stubbornly.

"I think there was."

"Where was it? We searched this house for one. We didn't find it."

When she did not answer he looked at her. She was sitting

still, her tired hands folded in her lap, her blue eyes sunken, the life gone out of her.

"I hate this job," she said. "I hate prying and spying. I'm through. I can't go on. I can't send a woman to the chair."

He knew her through long association. He realized that in her present mood he could not push her.

"It was a woman?" he said quietly.

She nodded.

"How was it done, Hilda?"

"It had to be done by someone who knew the house," she said slowly. "Someone who knew the light circuits. Someone who knew this radio and had a chance sometime to discover how to adjust the remote-control phonograph. It didn't need much. It could be done in a few minutes. After you find the blank spot on the radio, all you have to do after that is to turn the dial to that spot. Then you could start the record, and it would play here."

"Where was it played from just now?"

"There's a young man in Carlton's room," she said dully. "I promised him ten dollars to come tonight. I'd better pay him and let him go."

He gave her the ten dollars and she went out. She was gone a considerable time. When she returned she looked so pale that the inspector thought she was going to faint.

"He left the machine," she said. "He'll get it in the morning. If you want to see it—"

"See here, I think you need some whisky."

"No. I'm all right. If you'll come along I'll show you."

She got up heavily and led the way. Carlton was still downstairs with Susie, but his room was lighted. Sitting on the floor by a base outlet was what looked like a small phonograph about a foot in diameter, with a record on it. It was plugged into the wall, and the inspector, picking up the record, saw that it was the Habanera from *Carmen*. He started it, and going to Mrs. Fairbanks's room switched on the radio. Almost immediately the Habanera started. He switched it off, and went back to Hilda. She was still there, standing by a window.

"How long have you known about this?" he demanded.

"Only today. Something Susie said. I saw the radio set where it is, and—I wondered about it. You see, there are almost no stations on the air at one or later in the morning, and when they are it's dance music. I had just remembered it was something from *Carmen* that night. I should have thought about that sooner," she added, and tried to smile.

He had an idea that she was playing for time. He was wildly impatient, but he did not dare to hurry her.

"You see, it didn't take long," she went on. "I've tried it. Two minutes was enough to use the knife and turn the radio dial to the blank spot. And the doctor was in Jan's room for five minutes, maybe more. Even at that she took a chance. A dreadful chance," she said, and shivered. "She wasn't quite normal, of course. Those bats and things—"

"Listen," he said roughly. "Are you trying to tell me that Ida did all this?"

"Ida? No. She used them, of course. Amos saw her in the cupola. I suppose she was given a reason. Maybe to get Mrs. Fairbanks to leave the house. Maybe something worse, to scare her to death. And she hid the machine in the loft of the stable the next day. She carried it out in some blankets. That was why Jan was hurt, and I was locked in. The machine was hidden there, behind some trunks, or in one, I don't know. It had to be taken away, of course. She was in the loft when Jan got there. She had to get out."

She looked at her watch, and Fuller at last lost patience.

"Haven't we played around enough?" he said. "What is all this? Are you giving someone a chance to get away?"

She shook her head.

"I don't think so. No. I—" She closed her eyes. "Ida had to die, you see. She knew too much, so she got arsenic in a cup of tea. In the sugar, I suppose. The way Mrs. Fairbanks got it. If it hadn't been for Ida—"

Downstairs the telephone was ringing. Hilda got up and opened the door. Carlton was talking over it in the library. He sounded excited, and a moment later he slammed out the side door. Hilda was standing very still, listening while the inspector watched her. Her eyes were on the stairs when Susie came running up. She was gasping for breath, and her eyes were wide with shock.

"It's Eileen," she gasped. "She's killed herself with Frank's service revolver."

Then, for the first time in her life, Hilda fainted. The inspector caught her as she fell.

27.

Two NIGHTS later Inspector Fuller was sitting in Hilda's small neat living-room. The canary was covered in his cage, and the lamplight was warm on the blue curtains at the windows and on the gay chintz-covered chairs. Hilda was knitting, looking— he thought—as she always did, blandly innocent. Only her eyes showed the strain of the past two weeks.

"Why did you do it, Hilda?" he said. "Why did you telephone her that night?"

"I was sorry for her," said Hilda. "I didn't want her to go to the chair."

"She wouldn't have done that. After all, a prospective mother—"

"But you see she wasn't," said Hilda. "That was her excuse to get into the house."

He stared at her.

"How on earth did you know?"

Hilda looked down at her knitting.

"There are signs," she said evasively. "And it's easy to say you have a pain. Nobody can say you haven't."

"But Garrison didn't deny it."

"What could he do? She was his wife, even if he hadn't lived with her for years. I suppose he had suspected her all along, after the arsenic. I knew he was watching her. He'd followed her there at night, maybe when she went to see Ida. In the grounds, perhaps."

"Then she knew about the agreement? That if Mrs. Fairbanks died the alimony ceased?"

She nodded.

"He must have told her. If they quarreled and she taunted him because he was hard up he might, you know."

"How did she get the arsenic into the sugar?"

"Maggie says she came to the house the day before Marian and her mother returned from Florida. Jan was home by that time. She came to see her. But Mrs. Fairbanks's tray was in the pantry, and she went there for a glass of water. She could have done it then."

"But the poison didn't kill Mrs. Fairbanks. So then it was the terror. That's it, of course."

"The terror. Yes. Ida had told her about the hole in the wall, and—I think she had something on Ida. Maybe an illegitimate child. There was a boy at the farm, and Eileen's people lived nearby. She'd have known."

"It was the boy who brought in the bats and the rest of the zoo, including the snake?"

"Well, I can't think of any other way," Hilda said meekly. "She may have told him she sold them, or something. Of course it was Ida who got Eileen the position as Jan's governess."

"And got a cup of poisoned tea as a reward!"

"She got the five hundred dollars, too. Don't forget that. In new bills that Mrs. Fairbanks gave Eileen the night before she was murdered. Maybe Eileen bought her off with them. Maybe she just kept them. I don't know. But she couldn't stand for the stabbing anyhow, poor thing. Remember how she looked the next morning? And she must have had the phonograph in her room while we were there. She must have been scared out of her wits. It wasn't until later that she took it to the loft, under the blankets, and hid it there."

"Where Eileen retrieved it the next night. And nearly killed Jan. That's right, isn't it?"

"Yes." Hilda looked thoughtful. "It's odd, but I saw her. I didn't know who it was, of course. I raised the window and she was across Huston Street. She pretended to be calling a dog."

He got up, and lifting a corner of the cover, looked at the bird. It gazed back at him with small bright eyes, and he dropped the cover again.

"You're a funny woman, Hilda," he said. "In your heart you're a purely domestic creature. And yet—well, let's get back to Eileen. How and when did she use this radio-phonograph? Have you any idea?"

"I knew she had it," she said modestly. "I found the man who sold it to her. She said it was to go to the country, so he showed her how to use it. As for the rest, I think she killed Mrs. Fairbanks and set the dial by her bed while the doctor was with Jan. Then he gave her the hypodermic and left her. That's when the music started. He was in the hall."

"Where did she have the thing?"

"Anywhere. Under the bed, probably. There's a baseboard outlet there. She let it play until Carlton went in and turned off his mother's radio. If he hadn't she would have stopped it herself. She didn't even have to get out of bed to do it. But of course things went wrong. I was there, in the hall. She hadn't counted on my staying there every minute. And Ida was busy with Marian. I suppose that's why she fainted when she did. She hadn't got rid of the machine, and I'd found the body. She had thought she had until morning."

"So it was there under the bed when you searched her room!"

"It was nothing of the sort," she said indignantly.

"All right, I'll bite. Where was it?"

"Hanging outside her window on a rope."

He looked at her with admiration, not unmixed with something else.

"As I may have said before, Hilda, you're a smart woman," he said, smiling. "My safe looks like a rummage sale. I'll present you with some of the stuff if you like. But I'd give a good bit to know why you interfered with the law and telephoned her."

"Because she hadn't killed Jan," Hilda said. "She could have, but she didn't."

"What did you say over the phone? That all was discovered?"

She went a little pale, but her voice was steady.

"I really didn't tell her anything," she said. "I merely asked her if she still had her remote-control radio-phonograph. She didn't say anything for a minute. Then she said no, she'd given it away."

There were tears in her eyes. He got up and going over to her, put his hand on her shoulder. "Oh, subtle little Miss Pinkerton," he said. "Lovable and clever and entirely terrible Miss Pinkerton! What am I to do about you? I'm afraid to take you, and I can't even leave you alone."

He looked down at her, her soft skin, her prematurely graying hair, her steady blue eyes.

"See here," he said awkwardly, "Jan and young Brooke are going to be married. Susie and Carlton Fairbanks are going on a second honeymoon, looking for a farm. And unless I miss my guess Frank Garrison and Marian will remarry eventually. I'd hate like hell to join that crew of lovebirds, but—you won't object if I come around now and then? Unprofessionally, of course, little Miss Pinkerton."

She smiled up at him.

"I'd prefer even that to being left alone," she said.

After he had gone she sat still for a long time. Then she determinedly took a long hot bath, using plenty of bath salts, and shampooed her short, slightly graying hair. Once more she looked rather a rosy thirty-eight-year-old cherub, and she was carefully rubbing lotion into her small but capable hands when the telephone rang. She looked desperately about her, at the books she wanted to read, at her soft bed, and through the door to her small cheerful sitting-room with the bird sleeping in its cage. Then she picked up the receiver.

"Miss Pinkerton speaking," she said, and on hearing the inspector's voice was instantly covered with confusion.

AMERICAN MYSTERY CLASSICS

from PENZLER PUBLISHERS